TOXIC

NICCI CLOKE

HOT
KEY
BOOKS

First published in Great Britain in 2018 by
HOT KEY BOOKS
80–81 Wimpole St, London W1G 9RE
www.hotkeybooks.com

This is a work of fiction. Names, places, events and incidents are either the
products of the author's imagination or used fictitiously. Any resemblance
to actual persons, living or dead, is purely coincidental.

A CIP catalogue record for this book is available from the British Library.

ISBN: 978-1-4714-0658-4
also available as an ebook

H

For Mum, for everything

Sometimes, you must wonder.

What it was like to be me that day. To wake up and to not know. To not remember.

Maybe you imagine it. We've all been there, after all. Waking up with that sinking feeling you get when you know that your memories are missing, that the pieces of the night which went before don't quite fit together. That twisting fear, the voice whispering, 'I don't know what happened to me.'

But you do know what happened to me.

You know because you were there.

HOPE

'C'MON, HOPE, LIGHTEN up!' he says to me, his hand closing round mine, and the rest of the boys laugh.

'You guys are disgusting,' I say, turning away, and that only makes them laugh harder.

To be fair, I can't help smiling either, even when Dev lets off another rancid fart next to me. It smells of rotten Egg McMuffin – unsurprising, given he ate three of the things on the way here – and would be an antisocial thing to do even if we *weren't* all stuck in a cramped plane with the air being recycled for the next five hours. But yep, I'm still smiling. Because we're finally off. We're finally on *holiday*.

JB, who's sitting across the aisle from me, seems to find it less funny. He's gone a strange greenish colour. Nate nudges him, probably about to make some snide remark, but JB lurches out of his seat, and just makes it to the tiny toilet in front of us before we hear him hurl *his* McMuffin back up.

This is also unsurprising, given that JB lost almost every round of the drinking game we played in the minibus taxi to the airport, and also got dared to down two dirty pints in the Wetherspoon's back at Stansted.

Some people say that girls and boys can't be friends, and with the combined smell of Dev's bumhole and JB's regurgitated breakfast mingling around me, I can understand why. But I've also laughed so much this morning that my stomach's already aching, and I'm feeling really glad that they invited me to tag along on their 'lads' holiday'. They've had it planned for months, and for a while, the girls were kind of planning one too. But that didn't pan out, because, well, reasons. And secretly I was glad. Lately there's been a bit of tension between a couple of the girls and it feels like we're starting to drift apart.

'Any drinks? Snacks?' The air hostess bumps her trolley back up the aisle past us. We're near the front of the plane – which has turned out to be lucky for JB – and I think she's a bit sick of us already. You'd think that the fact we have to pay for our drinks on this uber-budget flight might put the boys off ordering round after round. You would be wrong.

'Six Stellas, please!' Zack says, beaming at her and waving his credit card. He's always buying rounds. OK, so it *is* his dad's money, but still, he doesn't have to share, does he? It's like a job he's given himself in the group – always trying to make sure we're having a good time. The air hostess smiles at him – one of those smiles that's so tight at the corners and at the eyes that you know it's meant to be a *screw you* – and starts dolling out our cans of beer. My head's feeling a *little* bit fuzzy but not too bad; I managed to skip a couple of drinks in the cab and one at the airport and I've also been carb-loading like mad all morning. So actually I kind of enjoy the taste of this one, the way it fizzes over my tongue. I can feel my whole body relaxing as we fly higher, higher, away from England and the stress of AS exams.

The only slight kill to my buzz comes when I glance past

Dev and his cloud of weapons-grade gas and see Logan in his window seat. Don't get me wrong; me and Logan are cool. Now, at least. Well, actually we have been for ages. Almost a year. It definitely feels like the break-up was a long time ago anyway.

But still – it's never going to be easy, going on holiday with your ex, is it? Even though we're mates now, sometimes it's hard to forget that we've, you know, seen each other naked. And he's looking good at the moment. His smooth brown skin is a shade darker from the freak sunshine we had at home last week and he's let his hair grow out a little bit, the way I always liked it.

I guess that's the way Daisy likes it too.

'Hey, Hopey,' Zack says, leaning across the aisle and interrupting my thoughts. 'How's your first lads' holiday turning out?'

There's the sound of a fresh round of retching from the toilet and the boys all laugh. And even though it's totally gross, the beer is going to my head in a lovely, bubbly way, and I can't help joining in.

WE LAND AT Heraklion airport just after 3 p.m. Greek time, and are shepherded onto a waiting coach by Zack, who somehow manages to get his dad act on despite having downed about seven beers on the flight. It was Zack who organised the apartment too, but as we watch all the other groups of guys and girls boarding the coach – some of them in matching tour T-shirts with nicknames printed on the back, including a hen party complete with veiled (and hammered) bride – I'll admit that I'm sceptical about where we're going to end up.

JB, now perked up (and mouthwashed), sits down next to me, and as the coach sets off, we watch the rocky road ahead as we climb through dusty hills. Logan sits across the aisle from us, along with Nate, who's been quiet all day, while Zack and Dev have already started chatting to the two Welsh girls sitting opposite them.

'You excited then, Novak?' JB offers me the crumpled pack of Monster Munch he's just rescued from his bag. He needs to hurry. He's got about thirty seconds before someone notices and starts up the 'Eating's cheating' chant.

'Course,' I say, glancing out of the window as we hit some kind of main road. '*So* good to be away.' I reach out and pinch his cheek with its patchy attempt at stubble. 'We're free!'

He laughs. 'Sure are. Hey, sorry about your girls' holiday. Georgie was really disappointed.'

Georgie is JB's stepsister, and I get on really well with her. But things have been a bit awkward between her and Charlotte, one of our other friends, since Georgie started going out with Josh, who Charlotte's had a crush on since we were about nine. It's silly and I'm sure it'll all blow over – it's hardly a good reason to lose a friend. But I also don't think Georgie *was* that disappointed about our holiday plans not working out – I get the feeling she'd much rather spend the time with Josh, anyway.

But I just shrug, because that's easiest. 'Thanks for letting me tag along on yours.'

'Hey, any time, Novak. You've always been one of the boys.'

'Course she is,' Dev says, turning round and pressing his angular face through the gap between the seats. 'Hopey, I'm expecting you to be my wing-woman allllll week.'

'She's not a miracle worker, Devdas,' JB says, flicking Dev's nose.

I meet Dev's eye and wink. He needs this holiday, and JB knows it. Dev might be pretending he doesn't miss Mollie, who he broke up with a couple of months ago, but it's obvious he's still gutted. I don't know exactly what went on there, but Dev hasn't been the same for weeks. It's really good to see him in such a good mood today, back to the goofy joker he usually is.

I've known all of them since Year 7 – well, not *known* them, not really, because I came from the tiny little village school while most of them had gone to the big primary in town. I was cripplingly shy when we started at Dean Valley and so spent most of Years 7 and 8 in a spasm of panic and terror of being called on or noticed or in any way not invisible. It was only in Year 9 that I ended up in a maths class with Nate, Dev and Charlotte and got chatting to them about the sheer suckiness of SOHCAHTOA, after which we ended up sitting together. And then I started to get to know the others, at lunchtimes and stuff, and now we've just finished Year 12 and I can't imagine life without them. I love their stupid nicknames for each other and for me, and I love their stupid goofy jokes and their awkward hugs. The boys stink a lot of the time, but still. It's like having a whole bunch of extra older brothers. And since my actual brother decided to skip off to New Zealand for the next five years, that's been kind of welcome.

The barren road is starting to give way to civilisation: villas and abandoned building sites, everything bleached out in the bright afternoon light. The Welsh girls are still laughing at Zack's jokes, which is kind of normal. He has this way of talking to people – even if he's just met them – that puts them totally at ease. Making jokes but not *too* many jokes, interested but not *too* interested. He does it with boys as well as girls and the more time I spend with him, the more I wish I could do it too. He's the friend you always want to have in a group, the person who makes any awkward situation kind of fine.

Behind JB and me are a couple of girls who look a bit nervous about the rowdy crowd they've found themselves in the middle of – everyone chatting and singing and standing up to yell stuff at friends in other seats. I hear one of them mutter, 'I thought you said it was a chilled-out place,' but then I get distracted by the shots of some violent green spirit Zack is pouring out of a tall bottle he's pulled from I have no idea where, into plastic shot glasses he also seems have magicked from yet another pocket in his fancy holdall.

I think I'm quite drunk now.

The two girls behind us get dropped off first, at some gorgeous-looking hotel with pillars outside the front door and giant palms in the driveway. But the next group *aren't* quite so lucky. Their hotel is up a dusty drive with spiky, dead-looking plants filling a ditch along one side. We can't quite see the building properly from where the coach has pulled up, but the bit we *can* see is covered by scaffolding. The hen party get off here, looking annoyed, and a group of boys also have to get off, all of them jeering and jostling one of their friends, who was apparently in charge of booking their accommodation.

JB makes a pretend scared face at me. 'Hope Zack hasn't stitched us up.'

And he hasn't. We pull up outside Amiti Apartments ten minutes later. It looks freshly painted, brilliant white, with a bright orange sign beside the sliding doors. It's five floors high and I can just see the neon blue of a swimming pool behind the reception. It's nothing fancy, but it looks clean and, you know, finished.

We climb off the coach, Dev and Zack pretending not to be ecstatic that the Welsh girls – who are called Lucy and Rachel – are staying here too.

11

'Well in, Zack,' Nate says, looking up at the building and then through the glass at the pool. 'You've done all right here.'

'As usual,' Zack says, grinning, before following Lucy into reception.

'Are you guys here for a week?' Rachel asks, as we step into the cool of the lobby.

'Just four nights,' I say. 'The flights were really cheap that way.'

She nods. 'Yeah, we got cheap ones too – although our flight back is at like stupid o'clock on Tuesday.'

'You been here before?' Nate asks her, and she shakes her head.

'We went to Kavos last year, but we heard it was better here. More going on.'

'Yeah, our mate Zack found this page, Malia Unlocked,' Dev chips in, leaning on my shoulder. 'It has all the cool secret stuff listed – you should check it out.'

Rachel smiles at him. 'Cool, thanks.'

'All sorted!' Lucy says, skipping over with a form and a set of keys clutched in her hand. 'First floor, pool view.'

'Nice work!' Rachel smiles at us. 'Well, catch you guys later.'

'Yeah, we should all hit the strip together,' Dev says, although they're already halfway down the corridor. Lucy turns round and smiles, gives him a little wave.

'They're nice,' he says with a grin, once they're (just about) out of earshot.

'Very nice,' Nate says, clapping him on the back. 'Come on then, let's see what Zack's lined up for us.'

Zack pads over to us. 'Right, boys and girl, we're all set.

Someone call the lift – we're up on the third floor.'

We've been given three sets of keys – each with a fob for the front door afterhours, and a big gold key for our own door – one of which is immediately entrusted to me.

'Don't give Hope one,' Logan laughs. 'She's always losing stuff.'

He looks at me with this kind smile, that same twinkle in his eyes that I know so well. The look that says, *I'm only kidding*. That says, *I love you*. Except it doesn't, not any more. 'I trust her more than I trust Dev,' Zack says, also laughing, as the lift pings open and we step out into the third-floor corridor. Our apartment is right at the end, and we all stand outside the front door and watch Zack slot his key into the lock. He takes his time over it, turning to grin at us all like we're his kids. And that's kind of the way things are, Zack looking out for us. When Logan and I broke up, it was Zack who came and found me in the common room the next day, his hands full of packets of sweets from the vending machine. He sat next to me and he didn't ask if I was all right, just handed me the sweets now and then, and after a while he just said, 'You'll be all right though, won't you? You can still be friends?'

And he was right. We are friends.

'Honey, we're hooooome,' Zack says now, clicking the door open ceremoniously and letting it swing open.

It's probably a bit *too* much ceremony, to be honest, because the room inside is pretty basic. It's clean and tiled, a wooden-framed sofa in front of a wooden coffee table, three wicker chairs dotted around it too. There's a kitchen – well, a sink and two electric rings, a microwave, a tiny fridge and a couple of cupboards. The bathroom's there, through another door, and then, beside that, sliding doors out onto a little balcony, which we all crowd towards.

'The sofa turns into a bed,' Zack is saying, 'so one of us can kip out here.'

The hot air outside hits us in a wave as Nate slides open the balcony door. The pool is below, with its smell of chlorine and suntan lotion and damp towels. Beyond that are the grey concrete buildings of another, bigger hotel, and a scrubby bit of wasteland; behind that, in the distance, the sea.

'Ahhhh,' Dev says, taking in a lungful of pool air. 'Now this is what I'm talking about.'

On the other side of me, JB burps. It smells faintly of McMuffin. And Monster Munch.

'Let's take a look at the bedrooms,' I suggest.

There are two bedrooms, one with a double bed and a little fold-out camp bed, and the other with two singles.

'So obviously,' Zack says, in his most gentlemanly voice, 'Hope should sleep in here.' We're in the room with the two singles. 'And then whoever's not shagging can take the other bed each night.'

I mean, firstly: *Eww*.

But also: *What if I want to shag?*

'I can just stay on the sofa,' I seem to be saying. 'I'm the smallest, so that seems fair.'

I mean, sure, Hope. Give away all *your privacy – why not?*

Zack shakes his head in that over-the-top way he has, like a dog trying to get water out of its ears. 'No way, Novak. You're one of the lads but you're also one of the ladies, so you get an

14

actual bed, with the least amount of man-stink in the vicinity. That's just how it works.'

He's sweet – although I feel kind of confused being described as a lady and a lad; what the hell do either of those things even *mean* anyway? – and I don't want to be out in the living area, with the whole lot of them thumping back and forth to the bathroom all night. Plus the bedroom with the two beds has its own little balcony. Only a slice of one really, but enough for two people to stand on and look out at the sun setting over the hotel next to ours.

Plus – look, I'm not proud of it – I can't help thinking how Logan has a girlfriend and so won't be 'shagging'. So maybe, just maybe, it'll be Logan who ends up in the other single bed.

No. Hope. Seriously.

I can't think like that. Logan's my friend. *Daisy's* my friend, for God's sake, although how that's happened is anyone's guess. And I'm OK with it all, I am. It's just that he's here, and I'm here, and we're not at school and that, suddenly, feels just ever so slightly confusing.

It'll take time, I guess. That's what Zack said too, actually.

So I just shrug, and dump my bag at the end of one of the beds in the smaller room. The sun is starting to sink but only just, and I think ahead to tonight, butterflies turning in my stomach. The strip is a ten-minute walk from here, Zack said, and I can just picture it all sparking into life now, neon signs stuttering on, ice being shovelled into bars and fridges getting filled with bottles.

I wander back into the main room, and it's like we're all in sync because Zack says 'Well, apparently the strip doesn't get going till a bit later, so we should go for dinner and beers first. But that's ages away, so shall we just chill by the pool first? Get some cocktails in?'

And so we do.

IT'S ONLY WHEN I'm getting changed that I start feeling a bit weird about going out in front of all of them essentially naked. Bikini is basically naked, right? It's not *technically* naked, but with a touch of imagination to fill in the particulars, it's naked. I don't know, maybe it's just me, but I think it's always going to feel slightly wrong being in what is basically your underwear in front of a load of guys, good friends or not.

So when I first exit the little bedroom (which, so far, seems to be just mine), in my new bikini, a towel around me, I do feel insecure. It's not like I really want them to think I look *good* – it's just I'm a bit freaked out at the idea that they might be looking at all.

But none of them bat an eyelid. They're all in their swimming shorts, standing around with towels chucked over their bare shoulders.

'Ready, Hope?' Zack says, already gripping the door handle.

'Yup.' I pick up my key from where I left it on the coffee table, and I can't help raising an eyebrow at Logan. *See, I don't always forget things!* He grins at me, getting my message loud and clear. I'm glad to find that we still have that, that talking without speaking, the way you only get with the people you're closest to.

17

We pad down to the lift, flip-flops squeaking against the tiled floor. The air-conditioning isn't exactly futuristic, but it's still cool enough, and so when we're back on the ground floor, heading out of the huge sliding doors to the pool, the heat hits me again. I'm glad I packed factor fifty along with my more optimistic twenty.

The pool is packed with people splashing around and lolling with their elbows on the side. The white plastic loungers around the edge are also full, but as we step out onto the hot patio Zack spots a group starting to pack up in one corner. He marches over, his broad rugby shoulders pale beside the oiled bodies on the loungers. Within seconds he's chatting to a couple of the guys in the group like they've been friends for years, one of the girls standing up to join in as they all laugh at some joke he's made. He waves us over and we go, a dutiful little crocodile, to say hello to this group of friends from Swansea and take their still-sweaty loungers.

I settle into mine – Logan to my left, Nate on the right – and lean back, eyes closed, soaking up the warmth of the sun. There's music playing from speakers by the pool, some club number I half know, and everyone's conversations melt into one big blur of sound, a comforting kind of white noise.

'Hey, Hope, you got sun cream on?'

I jerk awake – realising, belatedly, that I've actually fallen asleep – and see Nate smiling at me from the edge of his lounger. He's wet from the pool, which means I've been asleep for longer than a second. I glance down at my legs, which are turning red. I swing them over the edge of the lounger and reach for my bag.

'Can I nick some after you?' Nate asks. The rest of our loungers are empty – I glance towards the pool and see the four of them over there, deep in a game of water volleyball with a bright pink inflatable ball that only travels a feeble distance through the air before sinking sadly back to the water.

I lotion up my legs and then the rest of me, rubbing extra into my face, which feels tight and hot. And then I offer the bottle to Nate, who takes it and squirts it directly onto his shoulders, rubbing it in with his long, elegant hands. He glances up and sees me looking – *where are my sunglasses?* – and he passes the bottle back after going over his face and the back of his neck with both hands.

I add another blob to my stomach, just to be sure. As I settle on my lounger, I can't help feeling a bit insecure again, because look at all these girls with their neon bikinis against their perfect airbrushed skin, glowing. No dry patches, no stray hairs, no cellulite. Does a tan hide cellulite? I know I'm not supposed to care about cellulite or stray hairs, and most of the time I really don't . . . But, I don't know. *Look* at them all. It's like I just dozed off and woke up in the middle of a magazine shoot or something.

I find my sunglasses beside me on the lounger; slide them on. That feels better. They're not rose-tinted but they do put a kind of gold sheen on everything.

Nate settles back on his own sunbed, water still dripping from its plastic slats where he first sat down. His footprints on the concrete are slowly evaporating. The music changes to an old tune, one I know and used to like, by an indie band who aren't really in fashion any more. Nate sings a line or two, putting his Ray-Bans on, and then he gets up again.

'I'm going to the bar, Novak – you want anything?'

I tip my head and look at him over the top of my sunglasses. 'Maybe. What you getting?'

'An ice cream and a beer.'

I reach for my purse. 'That sounds perfect.'

When he's gone, I think about how nice it is to be talking, and just *being*, with Nate. It's not like we fell out after me and Logan broke up or anything. It's just that we used to do a lot of stuff together, just the three of us, a lot of movie nights and hanging out at lunchtime and WhatsApping each other stupid jokes, and then me and Logan broke up and it'd have been weird to keep doing those things with Nate, so I kind of lost him too.

So yeah, it's nice. Things are getting back to the way they were and I think that's what I want.

Zack comes splashing over, water still pouring off him. He flops onto his sun-lounger and grins at me. 'Done all right, haven't I, Novak?'

'Yeah, it's great. Thanks for sorting it.'

'No problem. Right, I'm getting a disco nap in because tonight we are getting *on it*.'

He flips his sunglasses down from the top of his head and promptly falls asleep, arms crossed over his chest. The others slowly filter back too, bringing drinks from the bar. Dev's got two Magnums, both of which he eats before Nate's even returned with mine.

'Uhhhhh,' Logan says, dropping onto his lounger. 'The sun feels *so* good.'

20

'I know,' I say, just a tiny bit conscious of the fact that my boobs aren't staying exactly in line with the sides of my bikini.

He leans lazily over and raises his beer to me in a sort of cheers, before doing the same to Nate, who's finally returned with our drinks after failing to chat up the girl at the bar.

'Thanks, Nate.' The cold ice cream feels amazing in my mouth and, weirdly, is even good when washed down with a mouthful of sour beer.

Soon half the boys are asleep, while JB is engrossed in something on his phone and Logan is texting on his; Daisy, I guess. I slide off my lounger and go over to the pool. The sun is starting to dip towards the horizon now, and things are a little quieter, people starting to congregate around the bar instead of in the water.

I sit down on the edge and dunk my legs in. It's cool against my skin, washing away the beery drowsiness, and so I lower the rest of my body in. I look out at the setting sun and then back at my friends.

I smile and then I dive under the water and swim until my lungs feel like they're about to burst. When I break the surface and take my first gasp of air, I start to laugh.

THE STRIP IS heaving with people already, even though Zack said it wouldn't get *really* busy until after midnight. It's like nothing I've ever seen before – just bar after bar after bar, bright colours and flashing lights. Music thumps out of speakers while people spill onto the street, clutching bottles and plastic cups of fluorescent-looking drinks. Everyone is smiling and laughing, and people in branded T-shirts are handing out leaflets and vouchers and grinning at groups, stopping them to try to tempt them into the bars. Within five minutes we get offered a free fishbowl, a free round of shots, then a free fishbowl *and* shots. Within seven minutes Zack has negotiated for us to get *two* fishbowls and a round of shots at a small bar with plastic chairs around bright yellow tables. The girl who brought us over, in a matching yellow vest top, lets go of Zack's arm and goes over to the bar. The barman, a guy not much older than us, with a full tattoo sleeve on one arm and some pretty oiled-up hair, nods and flips two empty fishbowls up onto the bar. I'm not close enough to see the names on the bottles he picks up, but plenty of their contents goes into the bowls.

Meanwhile the girl pours pink shots out of an unmarked bottle into glasses on a tray, and then winds her way back through the tables to give them to us. About half of the other

22

tables are full, most of them with people sitting around their own fishbowls, the coloured straws streaming out of them while the liquid – layers of yellow and orange and pink – slowly turns murky.

'Here you go, guys.' The girl plonks down the tray of shots. 'Enjoy! Fishbowls are on the way.'

'Thanks,' Zack says with one of his winning smiles. 'Right team, ante up!' He hands out the shots. We all grin at each other, all say, 'Cheers.' My shot is sugary and sharp in my throat, and the empty plastic glasses slam back onto the table like a drumbeat. My fuzzy drunk feeling from the pool has totally gone now – after a shower and a can of Coke and a bowl of pasta at the restaurant at the end of our dusty road, I feel properly awake and alive and ready to go. Buzzing.

When the fishbowls are delivered, I end up sharing one with Nate and Logan. I'd be quite happy to sit and sip it – especially as it tastes like a mix of orange and hairspray, not exactly appealing – but Zack, who's sharing the other one with JB and Dev, yells, 'Race ya!' and they start hoovering theirs up with about three straws each. I roll my eyes, but Nate nudges me and says, 'Come on, Novak!' and I find myself with three straws in *my* mouth, sucking as hard as I possibly can.

It tastes pretty disgusting, but when we win, when Nate and Logan high-five me, I get this warm feeling in my chest and I don't know if it's the booze or just . . . everything.

After the fishbowls, we carry on down the strip, half walking, half dancing our way between bars, until suddenly it's midnight and I am *drunk*.

I find myself by the bar with Logan, both waiting to be served. He has the sort of dozy look he gets on his face when he's pretty drunk, like everything around him makes him both sleepy and happy, and he grins when he sees me and puts an arm round me.

'I love this holiday already,' he says, raising his voice so I can hear him over the music.

'Me too.' I'm feeling pretty dozy myself, the heat and music thudding through me and Logan's skin warm next to mine. When he lets go to turn and order from the barman, I feel sad. *Stop that*, Sober Me (now a very small and quiet voice) tells Drunk Me.

'Another?' Logan says, gesturing to my empty glass, and I nod, fumbling for euros.

'Here.' He passes me my new drink and then waves my money away. He picks up his own and then, just as we're about to head back to the group, he looks down at me.

'I'm really glad you're here,' he says, and I feel warm all over again.

After that cocktail, things become a little broken.

We're dancing on a bar somewhere, Zack with his top off, all roaring along to '99 Problems'.

We're standing outside in the warm night, watching Dev get a henna tattoo after losing a bet with Nate. The bet was that Dev could pull a girl faster than Nate in the last bar we were in – I remember it being purple, the floor sticky, but

I don't remember a name or what we did there – and Nate completed the challenge in under five minutes. Zack, doling out the forfeit, has chosen the tattoo for Dev. It's a cartoon penis, and it's going on his bum. Dev pulled a girl too, just not quite as quickly as Nate. Otherwise the tattoo would have gone on his face.

We're dancing on a table somewhere, Logan, JB and me, and the table is not very steady. The bouncer looks angry. Zack lifts me down and throws me over his shoulder. He spins around until I think I might be sick from laughing.

He falls.

We both fall.

I'm still laughing.

There are more shots.

There are more fishbowls.

We are sitting at a table outside a place I don't remember, sweat cooling on our skin. Some of the boys are smoking and there are cold bottles of beer in front of us. A girl walks past in denim cut-offs and a suede bralet, and Dev makes the mistake of muttering aloud, 'She'd get it.'

'*Tell her!*' the others roar, and *Tell her* is the law.

Dev swears and hurtles off down the street. He taps the girl on the shoulder and we see his lips move.

The girl throws her drink at him.

I'm still laughing.

25

We are still sitting at a table outside a place I don't remember, and Dev's shirt is slowly drying. The beers are almost empty. A girl walks past in a black cut-out dress, slices of tanned hip showing through, and Dev makes the mistake of muttering aloud, 'Oh my days, she is fine.' But he's quicker this time – he glances up and remembers to say, 'Tell her,' just before the others say it and so he's safe.

The girl walks on by.

We are dancing on a flashing dance floor in a dark, dark bar where all our white bits glow blue. Dev is kissing the girl in the cut-offs and Zack is with a girl whose face I don't remember. Logan holds my hand and twirls me around.

'You caught the sun,' he says, and the music is so loud he has to come right up close to say it.

We're in McDonalds, ordering food. JB is outside McDonalds, throwing up orange and yellow and pink.

We're walking home, the laughter and the music and the smell of the strip fading behind us, hands greasy and speckled with salt, open burger boxes wobbling as we walk.

I am happy.

I am so happy.

I AM HUNGOVER.

I am so hungover.

I groan and throw the sheet over my head, trying to block out the bright sunlight that's flooding through the thin white curtains. My mouth feels dry and sticky and my eyes are still crusty with last night's make-up.

I turn onto my side and peep out from under the sheet. JB's in the bed beside mine, and I have a vague memory of the two of us sitting up in bed eating chips – yep, there are the empty cartons on the floor – and talking intensely about life. No idea what we actually *said* though – I vaguely remember him saying something about Josh not treating Georgie very well, and I wish I could remember it properly because it feels like it was important.

JB's flat on his back, snoring. He's clutching his phone, his hand flopped over the edge of the bed. I close my eyes, wondering if I can get back to sleep – with any luck, I'll feel better next time I wake up – but music starts playing from the pool outside. My eyes pop open again. I'm wide awake and I need a wee and my head feels like it's about to fall off. I throw the sheet aside again and get up as quietly as I can, padding barefoot around JB's bed.

Nate is asleep on the sofa in the living area, although he was obviously too drunk to unfold it into a bed – so he's scrunched up uncomfortably on it, his feet hanging over one wicker arm and his head propped awkwardly against the other. The other bedroom door is wide open and I can see Zack's stomach rising and falling as he snores, loudly, flat on his back, Dev curled on his side with a pillow pressed over his head. I can't see Logan on the camp bed on the other side of the room, but I imagine he's in a similar position – he hates snoring, although he's just as bad half the time. I sneak into the bathroom and close the door as quietly as I can – although I probably don't need to bother, given that Zack's currently drowning out most other sounds.

I sit on the loo, pressing my hand against my forehead as another bolt of pain throbs through my skull. Like an idiot, I didn't drink any water last night. That, plus mixing all those drinks . . . I've really only got myself to blame.

Bits of the night come back to me and I can't help smiling, thinking of Zack's goofy dad-dancing, Nate's one-liners, Dev trying to leapfrog a bin and tipping sideways into a bush. And then I'm smiling in a different sort of way, because I'm thinking of Logan's arm round my shoulders, Logan's face near mine.

Nope. Stop that right now.

I flush and then go to the sink to wash my face, scrubbing hard to get the dried mascara traces from under my eyes. I look at myself in the mirror. Ponytail half falling out and skew-whiff on my head; sunburnt streaks on my cheeks and collarbone. The rest of me stubbornly pale. I'll have to do a better job of putting on sun cream today. My stomach gurgles, which is a good sign – maybe I'll be able to kick this hangover with a fry-up and a pint of orange juice.

I jump in the shower while I'm still feeling all right, and by the time I come out Nate's pottering around in the living room and Zack's got the little plastic kettle boiling.

'Moooorning, Hope-Dogg,' Zack says. 'Sugar and a half, right? Just show it the milk?'

I grin at him. 'Spot on, Zack. Thanks.'

'Yeah, well, there's only three mugs,' Nate says, 'so you better drink it fast before that lot show their faces.' He reaches up and stretches, all the muscles in his chest flexing. 'God, I am *hanging*.'

I'm actually feeling pretty good now, especially after my first slurp of tea from the chipped plastic mug. I keep that to myself though. Nobody likes a smug face first thing in the morning, and besides, my hangovers have a tendency to creep back as the day goes on.

'Morning.' Logan leans against the bedroom doorframe, wearing just shorts and a sleepy smile. I have to look away.

'Mornin' Lo-Dogg,' Zack says. 'You are the lucky winner of the last mug. You mug. Milky, two sugars, right?'

I go into the bedroom to dress, my cup of tea warm in my hand.

We eat breakfast out on the patio by the pool. As suspected, my headache's back with a vengeance, but it retreats again briefly when my fry-up is put in front of me. It's properly greasy, bacon pale and fatty, the sausage beige with a single burnt stripe on each side. And I get stuck straight in. I shovel the entire fried egg onto a triangle of cold toast and shove half of that into my mouth in a single mouthful.

'Bloody hell, Hope,' Dev says. 'That is impressive. It used to take Mollie about an hour to eat a bowl of cereal.'

I concentrate on forking beans onto the chunk of sausage I've sawn off and choose not to mention that Mollie has been worried about her weight since she overheard Freddie, Zack's older brother, saying she was 'pretty for a chubby girl' at Zack's birthday party two years ago.

'Urghhhhhhhhh,' JB says. He's sitting with his forehead resting on the table and he's been making that noise roughly every five minutes. His breakfast is a pint of Coke which is sitting in a slowly growing puddle of condensation as the ice melts.

'I feel you, man,' Nate says, pushing his breakfast away and slurping up the dregs of his pint of orange juice. 'My head is *banging*.'

'Pull it together, boys,' Zack says, reaching over to grab the sausage from Nate's plate and eating the majority of it in one bite. Zack never seems to get hangovers. I've known him to go and play rugby while everyone else has still got their head stuck down the nearest toilet. 'You've got about an hour before Operation Get Back On It begins.' He tosses the last bit of sausage into his mouth. 'In fact, I fancy a beer now.' He signals to a waitress. 'Hope, you in?'

There's something about the way he looks at me, like he knows I'm going to say no. There's something about the way Logan looks at me, with a small smile like he's pretty sure

30

I'll say yes. And I'm just the right amount of hungover for it to seem like a good idea.

'Yeah, all right,' I say, enjoying the surprise on Zack's face although it doesn't last long. He waves to the waitress and then turns to the rest of the table. 'Well, come on then, lads,' he says. 'Who else is man enough?'

I don't really understand what having a penis has to do with being able to drink a beer with breakfast, but I'm distracted by the fact that Logan is scowling at his phone. After typing out a text, he slams it face down on the table then leans back in his seat. 'Count me in,' he says.

'You OK?' I ask, while the others are distracted by JB legging it to the disabled toilet on the other side of the restaurant. Zack and Dev stand up and jeer at him, while the waitress waits patiently for the order.

'Yeah,' Logan says, sounding anything but. 'Some things aren't meant to be, right?'

I hate that my first reaction is just a tiniest glimmer of hope. I remind myself that Daisy is my friend. I remind myself that *Logan* is, and that he's upset. I reach out and rub his arm. But what am I meant to say? I don't really know anything about their relationship.

Luckily the others are sitting back down now, and the waitress is pretty quick at delivering beers to Zack, Logan and me, and another orange juice to Nate. Now that it's in front of me, beer at this time of the morning – although, when I check my watch, it's actually just gone midday – doesn't seem like such a great idea. There's a whole afternoon and most of the night to get through . . . But I figure I'll just eat lots throughout the day

31

and pace myself. Besides, we're on holiday. This is the whole point of being on holiday, right? Having fun. Treating myself.

The next time the waitress passes, I order a piece of cheesecake.

I like holidays.

THE SHOWER FEELS good on my hot skin, sand sticking to the tray as the water trickles down the drain. I glance down to check out the sunburn situation and it looks like I've done OK today with the sun cream – just a weird red-lined finger-streak under my left boob where I've obviously missed a bit. My face feels hot and tight but I think that's from the salt and the wind – JB and I walked right down the beach, just chatting about school and things, to get to an ice-cream stall someone told Zack about. It was nice actually, looking out at the sea and just talking about *stuff* – about funny things that happened last night but also about Year 13 and exams and what happens after all that. JB is really good to talk to. I kind of wish I remembered more of what we said last night.

I switch off the shower and squeeze the water out of my hair, which feels like knots on knots. It's going to be *really* fun trying to comb this out. But then I see that someone has thoughtfully poured a vodka and Coke into a plastic cup and left it outside the bathroom door. I pick it up and take a swig. Hmm. A bit too much vodka and it doesn't taste *quite* like real Coke, but it's still quite sweet and refreshing, given I was starting to flag a bit.

Nate and Dev are ready to go out and sitting in the living

room, playing Shithead with a battered deck of cards on the little coffee table. It's a game I've always been good at – hoarding up my power cards and picking the exact right moment to drop them on someone else – but I know from past experience that Nate is even more ruthless than me.

Someone's playing music on travel speakers in Zack and Logan's bedroom, and there's the smell of deodorant and hairspray and aftershave drifting out. As I pad into my room, JB strolls out, wearing a neon Hawaiian shirt and drinking from the novelty plastic glass he stole from the Flamingo Cafe where we had a cheeky drink on the way back from the beach. He's also carrying his phone, which is playing Drake at a pitiful but valiant decibel level.

'Just farted in there,' he tells me, raising his voice to be heard over the two competing tracks and the yells as Nate decides to 'shit' on Dev. 'Soz, babe.'

Nate and Dev laugh at this, and Nate deals out a hand for JB to join them. I carry on into the bedroom, feeling a bit annoyed at JB – that was so put on for the others, he'd never have said it if it was just me and him. I close the door behind me and then crouch in front of my suitcase, fumbling through my clothes. I settle on a grey T-shirt dress and flip-flops because I'll be comfy in that, and right now I feel lazy and relaxed. Yeah, last night there were loads of girls dressed up, and maybe if I'd been with the others like we'd originally planned I would've felt like I had to as well. But I'm with the boys – they don't care what I'm wearing.

Apart from Logan maybe, that evil bit of me whispers, and that's all the more reason to wear the plainest thing I have.

I'm going to kiss someone tonight, I tell myself. Someone who gives me that little sparky looping feeling in my stomach, someone I don't know. That's what I need – I need reminding that there's a whole world outside of Kings Lyme and even Malia and that I can be whatever I want to be if I meet someone new. I comb out my wet hair and finish my drink as I put on some make-up. When I go back into the living room, Zack and Logan are out and ready too.

'Guys,' Zack says, standing up and looking at his phone, 'someone's just posted on the Malia Unlocked page about a booze cruise tomorrow – we're game, right?'

JB pulls a face. 'I get seasick.'

Zack reaches out to ruffle his hair, messing up what probably took a not inconsiderable amount of time and product. 'It's not exactly sailing the high seas, Popeye. It's a huge fancy yacht that moves at about half a mile an hour. They take you to some tiny little island, throw a party on the beach and then bring you back. Fifty euros each. It'll be bants.'

'Yesssss, boi,' Dev says, pouring himself an extra inch of vodka. He's wearing neon blue Wayfarers even though we're indoors, and an equally neon orange vest. He's a big fan of brights. 'Sounds sick.'

'Yeah, sounds good,' Nate says, but he's also looking at his phone and seems distracted. He frowns at the screen and then flips it round to show Logan. I can't see what's on there, but Logan's smile drops. He studies whatever it is for a second, then pushes the phone back to Nate and downs the rest of his drink.

'I'm in,' I say, going the rest of the way into the room and sitting down next to Dev.

'Yes, Hope-Dogg!' he says, high-fiving me. I pour myself a new drink.

'Cool,' Zack says. 'Booking tickets now. Hand your cash over.'

I hand over the contents of my purse to him – I'll have to go back into the bedroom and get some more out of the balled-up pair of socks in my suitcase. Fifty euros is a quite a big chunk of my holiday money – the money I spent hours waitressing at Starburger in town for. I think my hair will always smell just faintly of chip fat, but it was worth it, because here I am, on holiday with my friends for the first time ever.

And this boat trip sounds like the perfect way to celebrate.

AT OUR THIRD bar of the night, I realise two things.

One, I get drunk *really* fast when I don't eat dinner.

Two, Logan is flirting with me.

It starts with jokey hugs and arm-punching, because Logan isn't very good at flirting. And it seems like he's on a mission tonight, ordering shots and buying rounds before the rest of us have even got halfway through the first one. It's not long before he starts getting his goofy drunk smile, and it's round about then that he ends up next to me at the table. Dev and Nate are off getting cash out and Zack is scouting around trying to find a girl JB 'likes the look of', so it's kind of nice when Logan sits down next to me and drunkenly bumps his drink against mine in a cheers for like the third time tonight.

'It's great, isn't it?' he says, leaning closer to be heard over the music, his breath hot against my skin.

'Yeah, it is.' I can feel his eyes on me and I try – I *really* try – not to look up. But I can't help it. I've always loved his eyes. They're brown, but if you look close they have these flecks of green in them – just a couple. And right now they're fixed on my face, looking at me *properly*, the way you don't really look at someone who's just your friend.

'I don't want to go home,' he says, still looking at me, and I want and I don't want to say, *What about Daisy?*

'Loges!' Zack says, leaning forward on the table. He's grinning but I can see something else in his face, as if he doesn't really like us talking, as if he's picked up on the fact that we're getting closer again. 'Shall we get moving after these? Get the fishbowls in somewhere?'

Logan nods, although I don't really feel like he needs a fishbowl right now. 'Sounds good – right, Hope?'

My heart does something weird when he links us together that way – like we're making decisions as a pair, how we used to. So I nod too.

As we leave the bar, Zack puts his arm round me and leads me ahead of the others. 'Come on, Novak, use your skills to get us the best deal somewhere.'

But I can't help glancing back at Logan. And I can't help noticing that Logan is looking at me too.

Nate and Dev catch up with us on the strip, and by the time we decide on Rodeo, this massive bar we were in last night, Logan has somehow ended up next to me again. Rodeo is absolutely heaving, people pushing towards the bar and the buckin' bronco in the centre of the room, and as we climb the steps to its open front, a group of lads comes barrelling out, whooping. Logan pulls me out of the way – and into his chest – just in time to stop them knocking me back down the stairs.

It all happens quickly, and it's no big deal really. Except everything seems to go slow for a second, so that I'm incredibly conscious of Logan's chest against mine, of his familiar Logan smell and of his hand sliding down my back.

'Easy, Novak!'

I step away from Logan, and Zack is standing there, grinning. 'No fishbowls for you if you can't even stand up already!'

I roll my eyes at him and carry on into the bar, but my pulse is racing. It sounds so stupid to be going crazy because a guy has run his hand down my back, but all these memories are flooding in. Logan and me lying on the sofa watching telly; standing outside college with our crap coffees from the canteen; pressed against the wall at someone's party that we couldn't wait to leave.

I shake my head like I can actually physically force the thoughts out and go over to JB, who's leaning on the bar watching the guy make us two fishbowls.

'You OK?' I ask, because he's been quiet tonight, not quite himself.

'Hmm?' He glances up in surprise – I didn't realise he was so deep in thought. 'Yeah, yeah, good, hun. Just flagging a bit. This'll help, right?' He nods towards the fishbowls, which are a gross lurid yellow.

I pull a face. 'Um, yeah?'

He laughs. 'Yep, thought so!' Taking his chance, he reaches out to lift one of the bowls. 'Can you grab the other one?'

I follow him over to the spot the others have found for us to stand in, with a narrow ledge to balance the fishbowls on. Zack has his arm round Logan and is yelling something in his ear. Dev's still wearing his Wayfarers even though it's so dark in here he can't be able to see more than about two inches in front of his face, only a couple of moody red light bulbs hanging above us.

When we've put the drinks down, I nudge JB. 'Want me to be your wing-woman tonight?'

He laughs. 'You're all right, babe. I've got it covered.'

He still doesn't really seem himself, but I don't push it. I take a straw and offer him another, and we have a good long glug on one of the fishbowls before the others notice. And then Logan bumbles over and takes the straw out of my mouth.

'Hey!' I say, and he grins and slips it into his instead. When he lifts his head again, he puts an arm round me. 'Sharing's caring, babe.'

I elbow him in the ribs and grab another straw. JB's drifted off to talk to Dev, so for a while Logan and me just drink and bob to the music, completely comfortable in each other's company.

It hasn't always been like this. In the weeks before we broke up, things got kind of stiff and awkward between us. I still can't figure out what happened there. Logan can be really open and calm, but sometimes he gets quiet. He's not big on confrontation, and whenever we argued about anything – stupid stuff like what film to watch or who was supposed to call who – he'd prefer to just forget about it rather than talk it over. I dunno, I'm not big on confrontation either, but it kind of started to get on my nerves a bit.

'It's nice that we can do this again,' Logan says, reading my mind like he tends to do. 'I missed having you around.'

I smile at him, and I'm just drunk enough to say: 'Yeah, I missed you too.'

'Hey, how's your brother doing?' he asks, fumbling his straw towards him and taking a sip. I can tell by the way he's taking real care over each of his words that he's pretty hammered. I should probably be going easy on the fishbowls too.

'He's good,' I say. 'He's having a great time.'

'It was Queenstown, right?'

I'm weirdly pleased he remembered. 'Yeah. He's working in a hotel and getting free runs on the slopes whenever he wants, basically.'

'Cool. God, I'd love to go skiing again. That was so much fun, right?'

I smile and look away. He's talking about the Year 10 trip to Chamonix, and it *was* fun. It's also where me and Logan first got together. I can't help feeling like maybe he's thinking about that moment too.

'What was fun?' JB asks, appearing next to me again. I glance round and see Dev talking to a group of girls, his arm round one of them. As I watch, Nate heads over there too.

'Chamonix,' I say, turning back to the boys. 'We were just talking about Olly getting all his free skiing and thinking about how fun Chamonix was.'

JB screws up his face. 'Yeah, that whole trip was kind of tarnished for me by the chairlift incident.'

Logan and I both crease up laughing. I remember 'the chairlift incident' well – me and Logan were in the chairs behind JB and Charlotte as he hung over the edge and threw up. It was after a bit of a heavy night on the Jägers, hidden in the boys' dorm, and Mr Penney was *not* impressed.

'Looks like our boy still needs a bit of practice,' Zack says, coming up behind us with a tray of shots. I look in the direction he's pointing in time to see Dev wandering back over, the girls disappearing into the crowd.

'They had to go,' he says, shrugging, when he reaches us. 'I'll catch up with them later.'

'Yeah, OK, Romeo,' Nate says, patting him on the back. 'Come on, get a shot down ya.'

A while later, after dancing with Dev and JB on the packed floor, I'm too hot. My dress is stuck to me and my hair is plastered to the back of my neck, so I decide to slip out and get some air. It's good timing too, because Dev's just bumped into Rachel and Lucy, the girls from our hotel, at the bar, and now he and Zack are both desperately trying to impress them with increasingly ridiculous stories. So nobody notices when I step away for a minute.

It's not exactly cool outside either, but sitting on the metal steps leading up to the bar, there's at least a bit of air moving around me. I'm feeling drunk but also buzzy and good – probably from the approximately fifteen kilos of sugar in every fishbowl.

'Hey.'

Logan has followed me outside and I wish, I *wish*, that that didn't make my heart do a little flip-flop.

'Can I join you?'

I nod. 'Yeah, course. I was just getting some air.'

He sits down next to me and, just for a second, he leans against me, watching a group of girls pass with their arms thrown round each other, singing Beyoncé at the tops of their voices and totally unbothered that they're not in time or in tune or getting the lyrics right.

'I'm so drunk,' he says, that goofy smile on again. 'I swear, I'm never going back to Kings Lyme again.'

I smile. People spill out all over the strip in front of us, the air full of laughing and singing – and even though there's a smell of sick and beer and drains, it feels like freedom. It feels like school is a thing that happened ages ago and suddenly our whole lives are in front of us and we can do anything we want.

And I know what both of us want.

So when Logan turns his face to me, that smile still there, I lean in. Our eyes lock and mine close and I lean in for the kiss that has been coming all night.

The kiss that doesn't arrive.

'What are you doing?'

When I open my eyes, Logan is still looking at me. *Staring* at me.

And the smile is gone now.

'I THOUGHT . . .' The words won't come out, because suddenly I don't know what I thought. I feel completely sober, like I've floated up out of my body and I'm looking down at the two of us standing here. I'm realising that this whole time Logan actually did think we were just friends – and that this whole time I've been kidding myself that we could be.

I stand up. 'Sorry. One fishbowl too many.'

Logan winces. 'Hope, don't do that.'

'Don't do what?'

'You don't have to make excuses. I'm really sorry if I made you think something was going to happen.' He stands up, looking totally gutted. 'I'm all over the place tonight. Honestly, I'm really sorry.'

I turn away, my face burning. This is *humiliating*. 'It's fine. Jesus. It's no big deal.'

'OK.' Logan doesn't look like it's OK. 'Look, Hope, I love that we're hanging out again. I love having you in my life. But I'm –'

'Yeah, yeah, you're with Daisy, I *know*. Seriously, Logan, don't cry about it – I was just having fun, it's no. Big. Deal.'

And I walk back into the bar as if any of that is true.

* * *

It's hard to concentrate on anything that happens after that. My thoughts fly around and bump into each other and all these feelings keep rushing through me – one minute I'm embarrassed and the next I'm sad, because Logan doesn't see me that way any more. And then I'm angry because I swear it *wasn't* just in my head – and then I remember him standing there on the steps and I'm embarrassed all over again.

The only thing that will drown it all out is booze. That much is obvious.

And so I drink. I buy another round of fishbowls and I drink one pretty much to myself. I buy a beer and then a vodka and then a bottle of something blue and sweet. I stand by the bar and drink, and when I finish my bottle and a guy standing at the bar asks if he can buy me another, I say yes.

Later, when some other guy asks if he can buy me a shot, I say yes to that too.

And when Zack comes over and tells me that they're calling it a night – 'Gotta save ourselves for tomorrow, Novak! Booze *cuh-ruise*, my little friend' – I pull a pouty face. I say 'I don't *want* to go home yet! We're on holiday!' and I pretend not to see them all glancing at each other. I'm slurry and screechy and I do not *care*, because my plan has worked and I can't even remember how it felt when I leaned in and Logan did not kiss me.

'You know what, she's right,' Nate says suddenly, and I point at him and cheer.

'I'm game for a few more,' Dev says, and I give him a double point and a whoop. I have to keep moving around, because if I stop, the room spins a bit.

45

Zack has a face like thunder but he tries to hide it. 'I just think let's be chill,' he says. 'It's 2 a.m. already. Tomorrow's going to be shit if everyone's hanging out their arses. We're only here for four days, and it's blatantly gonna be the best one – I don't want us to waste it.'

Zack gets a long pantomime boo from me. People are starting to look.

'Yeah, I think Zack's right,' Logan says, folding his arms. 'C'mon. Let's go get a KFC and go home.'

I blow a long, fairly spitty raspberry and then turn to the bar. 'A fishbowl, please!' I yell at the nearest bartender, and then I turn round and say, 'Cool, *bye* then,' in the general direction of Zack and Logan. It's quite hard to focus at this point, so I concentrate on watching the barman.

By the time I turn back round with the fishbowl, Zack, JB and Logan have gone and Nate and Dev are leaning against the wall, talking to a group of girls.

I go over, sloshing some of the fishbowl onto my feet with a little 'Oops!' Dev turns round as I plonk it onto the ledge beside him and immediately stuff a couple of straws into my mouth.

'Wow,' he says, laughing. 'I love this wild side of you, Novak!'

I don't stop drinking to answer, just nudge a couple of straws in his direction. When I finally come up for air, half the fishbowl is gone.

'Hi,' I say, sticking my hand in the face of the girl closest to me. 'I'm Hope.'

'Naomi,' she says, shaking it. 'Having a good night?'

'Yep!' If I say it enough, it'll probably start to be true. 'You?'

'Yeah.' She leans closer. 'It's actually my birthday!'

46

'Oh my God!' I grab Dev's arm and look around for Nate, who's in deep conversation with one of the other girls. 'Guys! Guys! It's Naomi's birthday! We *need* more fishbowls!'

We end up in another bar after Rodeo, although I can't remember how we got there or why we left. Dev has hooked up with one of Naomi's friends, Jess (or it might be Jen, the music is quite loud and my memory is not working its hardest for me) and the two of them have decided to go for a walk on the beach. Naomi is holding my hand and asking me if I want some water, but I keep shaking my head and asking for a shot. Nobody seems to be listening to me, so I go to the bar and order one for myself.

By the time, we get to our sixth bar of the night, I realise two things.
    One: I am going to be sick.
    Two: Right now.

I RUN OUT of the bar and just about make it into an alleyway before three fishbowls, four beers, several blue drinks and too many shots make their way out of my mouth and splash onto the ground in front of me.

I stand with my hands on my knees, acid burning my throat. Just when I think I'm done, another huge wave comes rushing out of me.

And then I *am* done. I spit and straighten up, wiping my mouth with the back of my hand.

'Nice.'

I spin round. Nate is standing there, arms folded. 'You OK?'

I glare at him. 'You know it's not usually a good idea to follow a girl into a dark alleyway, right?'

He holds up his hands. 'Yeah, fair point. I just wanted to check you were all right. Come on, let's go and get some water.'

I follow him back onto the strip and to a little 24-hour minimarket thing, but the smell of the bars and the gutter makes my stomach lurch again.

'Might just wait out here,' I say to him, trying to breathe through my mouth and not lose the last of my stomach lining in front of the whole of Malia.

Leaning against the shop front helps, the glass nice and cold against my back. At least things aren't spinning any more – in fact, I think my hangover is kicking in already. My head is starting to pound, so when Nate appears with a litre of water, paracetamol, a loaf of bread and a bag of crisps, I want to hug him.

Due to being splashed with sick, I refrain.

'Come on,' he says. 'Dr Nate to the rescue.'

'Don't you want to go back and see those girls?'

He frowns and shakes his head. 'Nah. Not really into one-night things.'

This is news to me. If Zack's to be believed, Nate's slept with more people than the entire cast of *Geordie Shore*.

We reach a fork in the strip and Nate turns off and down a little slope towards the beach. That seems like a great plan – the music and the smell of the strip are too much for me right now – until we step onto the sand and see a couple *genuinely* shagging on a sun-lounger. Like properly going at it, her legs up in the air and his white bum bobbing in the darkness.

I burst out laughing and they stop for a second and then just keep going.

'Whatever floats your boat,' Nate says, heading away from them and further down the beach. There are a couple of people walking and another couple kissing in the sea, but otherwise it's pretty quiet. There's no sign of Dev and Jess/Jen. Nate pulls a sun-lounger up for us in front of a deserted hotel bar and we sit on the edge of it. I accept the bottle of water from him. My mouth tastes truly horrific so first I sluice it out and spit – as daintily as I can manage, which is not very – into the sand beside me. Then I take a good gulp and another, and it feels amazing – so cold and clean.

Nate has undone the bag of bread and he takes a slice, chucks in a few crisps and then folds it over into a makeshift sandwich and hands it to me.

I look warily at it. My stomach is settled for now, but it's still not happy with me.

'Trust me,' he says. 'First mouthful will be like sand, but it'll help.'

'I usually prefer my crisp sandwiches with extra mayonnaise,' I say. 'Ideally salt-and-vinegar crisps with some Stilton in there.'

Nate makes a fake gag face. 'Seriously. You're about to make *me* throw up.'

I take a bite of the sandwich and, although my body still isn't convinced eating is a good idea, I do start to feel better. The bread is that kind of crappy, chemical-filled stuff and really soft, and the crisps are extra salty. When I finish it, Nate makes me another one, and one for himself.

'Thanks for staying out with me,' I say.

'S'OK. Wasn't going to leave you with Dev.'

I take another big glug of water.

'You all right?' Nate asks. 'You've been acting kinda weird tonight.'

Part of me wants to bite his head off – *What, am I not* allowed *to have a good time?!* – but I know that's mostly because I'm embarrassed about earlier. And because it's still there, itching under my skin, I end up telling him exactly what happened with Logan on the steps outside Rodeo. I don't look at him as I say it, just at my feet burrowing into the sand.

'. . . and that's when I came inside and decided to get drunker than anyone's ever been, ever.'

I glance up at him, stuffing a big bite of crisp sandwich into my mouth in an attempt to make myself feel better.

Nate looks at me for a second, a kind of baffled expression on his face. 'I don't get it. What's the problem?'

'Well, now I've made things really awkward.'

'Hope, you still have feelings for someone you used to love. Sounds pretty normal to me. Don't beat yourself up.'

'Someone who has a girlfriend now.'

'Well, yeah, maybe that bit doesn't reflect all that well on you. But you'd had a drink, you made a mistake. And Logan's not exactly innocent here. He does still flirt with you – I'm his mate and I've seen it.'

Huh. Now I'm talking about it out loud, it doesn't seem that bad. I mean, it's still not fun to be rejected, but why should I beat myself up for putting myself out there?

'Thanks, Nate.' I take a handful of crisps. 'We should head back to the apartment, I guess.'

We walk back up the beach instead of going along the strip, just as the horizon starts to get lighter. We don't see anyone else shagging, thankfully, although there's a girl crying to another girl on a deckchair and a guy sleeping on a sun-lounger further down. As the sun comes up, people start wading into the sea, their faces and arms smudged with glow paint and stamps and stickers. The music from the strip thuds on and on and on.

When we get back to the flat, everything's quiet apart from the sound of Zack snoring. There are a couple of half-drunk bottles of beer on the coffee table, and a mug of tea, and JB has passed out on the sofa, which is a pretty standard JB manoeuvre.

'Come on, Goldilocks,' Nate says, heading over to him. 'You're in Daddy Bear's bed.'

But JB looks so peaceful, a cushion cuddled to his face, that I laugh. 'Aww, leave him,' I say. 'You can sleep in his bed, in with me.'

Nate shrugs. 'Yeah all right.' When we get to the bedroom door he grins at me. 'You're not gonna try and kiss *me*, are you, Novak?'

I punch him in the back and then I go and collapse into bed. I'm asleep before Nate even turns the light off.

AS SOON AS I wake up, I know it's late. The sun is streaming through the open window and I can hear people splashing in the pool and laughing, bottles and glasses being clinked in the bar. I sit up, noticing with some relief that my hangover's nowhere near as bad as I thought it would be. I glance over and Nate is still asleep, flat on his back with his head propped up against the headboard and his hands folded neatly over his bare stomach. A very *toned* stomach, I can't help noticing. I look down at myself, still in the dress from last night – and still ever so slightly sick-splashed. Lovely.

I get up and grab my towel from the floor. A shower is top of my priority list right now. I feel like once that's out of the way, I might actually feel all right. And I tell myself – very sternly – that I'm not going to feel bad about the whole awkward Logan thing. I made a mistake, and that's OK. I don't have to feel embarrassed about it. I'm not going to let it ruin the holiday I spent all those Saturdays flipping burgers for.

When I open the door, the others are all sitting there.

Staring at me.

'Morning,' I say, bright and breezy. *Not* embarrassed. It's not like anyone else knows what happened anyway, unless Logan's turned into an utter dickhead overnight.

'Moooorning,' Dev says in a low voice, with a weird, sort of suppressed smile.

Logan is staring at his phone with the kind of focus that makes me think he'd rather be looking anywhere but at me. And JB seems pretty awkward too, playing with the fringe on the edge of the cushion.

'You guys OK?' I ask.

Zack puts down his mug of tea and smiles at me. 'We're fine, Hope-Dogg. We're a *bit* surprised at the pair of you, yeah, but you know – what happens in Malia stays in Malia and all that.'

Wait, what? Is he talking about me and Logan? Nothing *actually* happened – surely that's not what they're all being so weird about.

'Where's lover-boy?' Dev asks with a wink. 'Too embarrassed to face the music?'

'What are you *on* about?' I feel like I've woken up in a parallel universe or something.

'We're on about Nate, babe,' Zack says, getting up and filling the kettle. 'Or Judas, as I like to call him. Do you want a cup of tea?'

'Nate?' I actually laugh I'm so relieved. 'Nothing happened between me and Nate! Are you for real?'

Zack does a big over-the-top shrug, like *Whatever you say*. 'It's just, you know, guy suddenly ends up in a room with a girl with the door closed . . .'

'. . . And they go to sleep just like any other pair of friends?' I say, folding my arms across my chest. I can't believe this. 'Like the exact same thing me and JB did the night before?'

Zack turns back to the kettle, keeping his stupid smug *Sure thing* face on. 'Just seems strange, babe. That's all we're saying.'

'JB was asleep on the sofa!' I say, starting to shout now. 'What were we meant to do?'

The kettle clicks off. Logan still hasn't looked up from his phone. 'Course, babe,' Zack says, and I swear I could actually pour the contents of that kettle over his head I'm so mad. 'I mean, Dev had found himself a kind hostess for the evening so *his* bed was empty and available . . .'

Dev gives himself a little wolf-howl and then looks around for someone to high-five. JB reluctantly obliges.

'. . . but whatever,' Zack says, stirring in milk unbearably slowly. 'Like I say, what happens in Malia stays in Malia. Right! Tea's here. Best get a move on if you want a shower before the booze cruise. We've got to be at the dock in forty minutes.'

I'm too frustrated, too furious, to even get any words out. So I just walk into the bathroom and stand under the lukewarm shower, absolutely steaming with rage.

I know what they're like. The more I try to deny it, the more they'll rib me about it, especially Zack. Probably when Nate gets up and says the exact same thing as me, they'll drop it – as if his word is somehow better than mine!

I lather up my hair, hard, and the anger starts to fizz out of me. Maybe I'm overreacting? After all, this is how they talk to each other all the time – always teasing each other and going totally over the top. Telling Dev how he can't get a girlfriend or telling Nate exactly how much they all want to do totally disgusting things to his mum. They all get a turn at being ribbed, and they all just accept it. That's just how their friendship *works*, I guess. Maybe this is all just a part of me being one of the lads now. Part of the gang.

It doesn't feel very fun though. I sigh and turn so that the water runs over my face. As *if* me or Nate would do that to Logan.

I wonder if he'd even care.

I suppose at least we've got today to look forward to. All of us hanging out on some fancy giant yacht, with free cocktails and pumping dance music, and then an amazing party on our own private island. A world – a whole *galaxy* – away from Kings Lyme.

IT'S NOT EXACTLY the luxury experience I was expecting. When we turn up at the dock, there are crowds of people waiting to board the boat, and half of them look like they're still up from last night – there's plenty of smudged glow paint on show, and red eyes and bleary voices. People are leaning on their mates and some are singing and the whole vibe is less glamorous yacht party, more rowdy football match.

The boat, by the way, isn't very glamorous either.

I mean, I'm not exactly an expert, but it's not the kind of thing you see celebrities lounging on in magazines. It's . . . a bit smaller than I was expecting, and although it *used* to be white, it's now sort of rust-stained with a massive splash of something greenish-yellow down one side. Dance music blares from speakers somewhere while a guy dressed in a leopard-print vest and baggy shorts is hosing down the deck. I don't even want to think why.

Things are still a little bit weird between me and Logan. Everyone else has sort of given up teasing me about Nate – I don't think any of them *actually* thought anything had happened; it was just Zack spurring everyone on because he thought it was funny. There's the odd comment, in a sort of wink-wink, nudge-nudge way but I'm just ignoring it now and

Nate doesn't seem that bothered either. When they don't get a rise, the boys soon get bored.

But Logan still hasn't really spoken to me, or to anyone in fact. He's been looking at his phone all day, and even when Zack and Dev try to get him involved in the conversation, he's kind of distracted and distant. I can't actually believe he'd think anything happened between Nate and me, but then maybe he's still feeling uncomfortable about the whole me-throwing-myself-at-him thing.

'Hmm, not exactly like they've borrowed the boat from Kanye, is it?' JB says, appearing next to me with two bottles of beer. 'Here, you'll need this.'

'Where'd you get these, you little genius?' I ask, taking mine gratefully.

'Some guy's selling them out of a bucket over there,' he says.

'Smart,' I say.

'Yeah, well, it looks like they'll be able to make good use of the bucket later,' JB says, gesturing towards the yellowy green stain on the side of the boat.

'Probably for you!' I say, laughing, and I give him a hug. 'By the way, I totally spewed my guts up last night.'

'I heard,' he said. 'Definitely a good thing – you'd feel like arse if you hadn't.'

'Yeah.' I glance at him. 'I was kind of a mess, wasn't I?'

JB shrugs. 'You were fine. No big deal, don't worry about it, babe.' He glances at me. 'You OK though?'

'Yep.' I take a big gulp of my beer, and I actually am OK. I'm not embarrassed and I'm not upset. I'm ready to have a really great day.

The boat still turns out to be pretty exciting once we get on it. Yeah, OK, it's not exactly top of the range or brand new, but there's a DJ with decks up on the highest level and a bar, and then down in the cabin there's all these beanbags and the lights are turned down (I decide it's probably best not to think about what that might be an attempt to hide) and there's another bar too. When we board we're handed a plastic cocktail glass full of a bright pink drink, and behind the bar I can see them loading up super-soakers with ouzo.

Making a mental note to avoid *them*, I turn away with my drink and bump smack into someone.

'Whoa, sorry!' I say, before I register it's Logan, now with bright pink spots on his white T-shirt.

'No, that was my fault,' he says, and we both look at each other for a second. It's definitely time to break the awkward ice here.

'Logan, I –' I start, but before I get any further, Zack comes barrelling over with one of the pink drinks clutched in each hand.

'Let's get this party started!' he yells, lifting both of them above his head, and all the people round us cheer. With perfect timing, the DJ suddenly whacks the volume all the way up, just as the motor of the boat starts to whine and we start backing slowly out of the harbour.

The party has officially started.

I find JB and Nate by the railings, looking down at the water.

'Hey, lover,' Nate says, and I punch him in the arm.

'Not funny.'

There's a shriek from the front of the boat, where a guy

with no top and very small shorts is bending a girl in a cut-out swimsuit backwards over the railings. He's laughing and she's struggling so hard that her feet leave the deck, one of her jewelled flip-flops coming off. 'I can't *swim*,' she yells, but all her friends are there, laughing, so nobody takes much notice. Maybe it's no big deal, but I'm glad when another girl comes strolling back from the bar and, rolling her eyes, kicks the guy in the shin. He lets her friend go and as soon as she straightens up, she pushes him – 'You *twat*' – but she's laughing too, so I guess she's OK.

I turn back and look at the beach getting slowly smaller as we head out to sea. The pink drink is surprisingly tasty and mine's gone before I even really notice.

'Another round?' Nate asks me and JB, and we both nod – although I can't help hoping JB doesn't get too drunk too soon. I'm not that hungover but I still don't fancy looking after someone who's puking this early in the day.

Dev comes bouncing over. 'How sick is this?' He hooks an arm round my neck and puts his face close to mine, his other hand stretched out to take a selfie. 'Hopey, I think we're actually in heaven.'

My flip-flops are kind of sticking to the deck in heaven, but his enthusiasm is pretty infectious. He starts dancing to the song, his actual lamest, stolen-from-the-Nineties dance moves – brushing imaginary dust from his shoulders to the beat, a spot of thunderclapping, a full Running Man – and soon JB and I are in stitches. When Nate comes back with the drinks, we end up in a kind of impromptu dance-off, all of us taking a turn to do our cheesiest moves in the middle of our little circle. I pull out a weird lunge-airpunch-combo to all-round approval, and it's only when I finish with a full-on knee-slide, like I'm six and at a wedding, that I realise we've drawn quite a crowd.

I don't even care; as Nate helps me up, I can't stop laughing. I feel full of energy, like totally *alive*, here on this grubby boat in the middle of the sea with my friends around me. The music is pounding and everyone is grinning and happy, talking to each other and singing along. Someone has taken advantage of the sudden cluster of people to crowd-surf, which seems fairly risky given how close we are to open water. Girls in T-shirts branded with the logo of the tour company, Party Boat, start working their way around the deck with trays of shots and I take one and neck it, totally not caring that it's about 2 p.m. and the whole day is ahead of us. Right now, this moment is all that matters, all I care about.

WE ARRIVE AT the island an hour – and several shots – later. The sun is high up in a bright blue sky and so far I've avoided having the ouzo-filled super-soaker shoved down my throat.

The others have not been so lucky. Logan, Nate and Dev are all sort of slouched against the railings, aniseed-breathed and dazed-looking, while JB (also ouzo free) is still bouncing around dancing with me and a stag party from Birmingham.

When someone taps me on the shoulder, I turn, ready to push away any kind of plastic weapon filled with alcohol. But it's Logan, a bit unsteady on his feet.

'Where's Zack?' he shouts, and I notice that even though he's quite drunk, his goofy drunk smile is nowhere to be seen.

'I don't know!' I yell over the music. 'I haven't seen him for a while.'

We're almost at the shore now, the boat slowing right down as the captain navigates us alongside the jetty. A girl clambers up onto the railings and yells something that *sounds* like 'Socks bitches are the best!' and then jumps over the edge into the water.

'Waheeeey!' Half the stag party are straight over the railing after her, three cannonballs hitting the water hard. I feel like it's a bit too shallow for that to be safe, but the mood is so high, and the pink drinks are warm in my belly, and it's kind of hard to worry about health and safety. So I just laugh with everyone else when I see Dev hurtle past, his vest (neon yellow today) getting discarded on the deck as he goes, but his Wayfarers still on his face. He does this weird kind of deer hop over one of the chairs at the edge of the deck and clears the railings easily, letting out a high-pitched whoop as he disappears over the edge.

'All right, no more jumping, guys,' a rep in a Party Boat T-shirt yells, walking towards the railings. 'It's kinda shallow now and nothing kills a party faster than a broken spine. Besides, there's still plenty of you who need to say *hello* to my little friend . . .' He brandishes his super-soaker, which is an offensive green colour and has clearly been recently refilled with Greece's finest aniseed annihilation. He pumps it a couple of times in a gross, graphic kind of way and then fires it at all of us. I shriek with everyone else as it hits me, although a girl next to me stretches up on her tiptoes and opens her mouth as wide as she can to catch the spray.

'It's not that bad,' she says when she sees me looking. 'And it's free, right?'

I think that sounds like pretty valid advice, so when we clamber down the gangway onto the jetty and there's a couple of bins full of beers and alcopops, I take a beer and then I take another one and wedge it in my bag.

The island is small and not exactly like the kind of cartoon desert island I was picturing. There's a bit of beach where we've just landed and then a building beyond that with toilets and what sort of looks like it might be a classroom or a canteen. The rest is kind of scrubby and wooded, the ground rocky and grey.

But there's a stage where the DJ from the boat is setting up, and the Party Boat reps are loading trays with beers and shots. Over to one side, two guys are setting up a keg with a siren attached. I kind of feel like I don't want to know what's going on with that.

I've lost the guys, who all raced on shore to wee in the 'privacy' of the straggly trees beyond the beach. To be fair, I'm not above what Zack calls 'squatting and squirting' (gross), but also wasn't above using the seen-better-days toilet on the boat – unlike those divas. I can pick out Dev's vest between the trees – seriously, there are NASA satellites that could pick out Dev's vest – but I've got no idea where the others are.

It's OK though, because I've still got that good buzzy feeling and it feels like everyone else does too. People are high-fiving and chest-bumping and kissing each other all over the shop, and it feels like some kind of special new community we're all setting up on this crappy little island.

Yeah, OK, maybe I'm a bit pissed.

We weren't moving that fast, out on the water, but without even that little bit of breeze, it's *hot*. There's a strong smell of seaweed, kind of cabbage-y, and a barbecue going at one end of the beach kicking up a *lot* of greasy smoke. The ouzo girl is next to me again and she looks approvingly at my extra beer.

'I'm Ness,' she says, grinning.

'Hope.'

'My advice is to steer clear of the chicken,' she says, nodding towards the barbecue.

'Noted.' I offer up my open beer in a cheers. 'Who are you here with?'

She gestures towards a group of girls already setting up camp on the beach. 'We just finished A levels.'

'Nice.' I raise my beer to her again, which is kind of lame. 'We just did our AS's.'

'Oh, babe,' Ness says. 'It gets so much worse.'

I laugh and we both drink to that.

'Hey, come meet the others,' she says. 'They've got a prime spot.' She squints at her friends. 'And it also looks like they've stolen a bottle of something extremely green from somewhere.'

I glance in the direction of Dev's luminous vest but I can't see it any more. I mean, it's an island – how far can they go? 'Yeah, sure,' I say, and I follow her.

Ness is tall and stunning – sandy blonde hair which is either natural or ridiculously good highlights, broad shoulders, the actual longest set of legs I've ever seen on a human before. And also unbelievably friendly, like pretty much everyone else in Malia – she spends the first five minutes introducing me to all of her friends, who are the nicest, most welcoming group of girls I've ever met. I get so many hugs that I lose track of everyone's names but they don't seem to care – they're already pouring me a plastic cup of the green stuff, which turns out to be melon-flavoured and delicious.

'Oh my God, you're the knee-slide girl,' Emily, the girl to my left, says. 'You're awesome!'

I laugh, embarrassed. Wow, this melon stuff really is delicious. 'Yeah, *might* have got carried away there.'

'Are those guys your friends?' she asks. She's wearing this

pretty, floaty kaftan sort of thing, with little silver beads that tinkle as she moves.

'Yeah, I kind of crashed their lads' holiday.'

She raises an eyebrow. 'No way? That's so cool.'

Is it? I didn't really think it was that big a deal.

'Aren't you a bit sick of talking about tits and farting?' one of the other girls, Hayley, asks me, reaching over to top up my glass. This melon stuff is sticky and thick; I think it's probably meant to be drunk with a mixer.

'A bit,' I say, laughing. But that feels kind of unfair. Yeah, the boys do talk about that stuff, but not all the time. I've had some really good chats, especially with JB and Nate.

'They're probably on their best behaviour, with you around,' Ness says, lying back on her elbows in the sand.

I shake my head. 'Don't think so. They're pretty used to me now.'

'You're one of the boys,' Emily says, and we all say cheers to that.

'Oh God,' Hayley says, looking in the direction of a group of Party Boat staff. 'Looks like they're organising a game.'

The game turns out to be a fifty-strong round of 'Never Have I Ever'. *I* have never really understood the point of that game – without a lie detector, why would you ever own up?! But somehow I find myself getting caught up in it all. Some of the stuff is over the top – 'I have never slept with my friend's mum' or 'I have never had a gang bang' or 'I have never slept with identical twins' – and others are clearly targeted at someone in particular – 'I have never had sex on the top deck of the

66

number 63 bus' or 'I have never pooed myself and blamed someone's dog'. Everyone gets a bit hysterical with laughing and sun, so when the more generic stuff comes up – 'I have never slept with a friend' or 'I have never had sex in someone else's bed' – everyone who *has* just drinks, obediently, as if there's no other possible option.

Dev works his way through the crowd, JB close behind, just in time for 'I have never been drunk in public' which gets a roar from everyone and a spontaneous drinks downing. Dev and JB manage to combine this with hugging me, which makes a sort of Hope sandwich with a side of spilt beer. The DJ turns the volume way up, so that the sand is practically jumping, and I've got Dev's breath hot in one ear – 'Where you been, babe? We missed yooooou' – and JB's in the other – 'Dev's pretty fucked up.' I give Dev's cheek a pinch while nodding to JB to show I've heard. He's right – Dev's pushed his sunglasses up on his head (of course, now that the sun's at its fullest and there's a legitimate reason to wear them) and his eyes are doing all kinds of weird things, pupils dilated and skittering about. He's singing along to the song really loudly, his fist raised in the air, and he looks like he's forgotten we're here.

'Did he take something?' I ask JB.

JB bites his lip. 'Yeah,' he says. 'We met these guys from Exeter in the woods. They had pills to sell.'

I roll my eyes. 'Seriously?'

'Yeah.' JB shrugs. 'C'mon, it's no big deal. It's not like we bought them from some random guy on the strip. These lads were really nice – they were like our age. They're on them too, it's totally fine.'

I open my other beer and take a sip, stalling for time. I don't know how to respond. It's not like I don't know the boys have dabbled with drugs before. Most of the girls too. We're from a small town, without much to do; people find ways of keeping themselves entertained. I hear them brag about the stuff they've taken at the weekend each Monday at sixth form.

I've never done it though.

It's not like I'm afraid of letting go – I've been drunk enough to streak through town; drunk enough to forget where I live; drunk enough to do things I can't remember the next day. But something about the idea of it scares me. I think maybe it's to do with losing control – at least when you're drinking, you can tell you're getting drunk. It seems like if you pop a pill, you just have to wait and see what happens. There's no turning back. That freaks me out.

Dev does look like he's having a good time, at least, although I can see his jaw moving back and forth, his teeth clenched.

'All right, party peeeeeeople!' It's Zack, never in need of a microphone, appearing beside us as the crowd melts away for him. He puts an arm round JB and Dev, enclosing me in the process, and when he pulls back I notice he keeps a hand just at the base of Dev's neck – casual and friendly, but in control. He's looking out for Dev, playing his daddy role. I wonder if he's taken any of the pills from the Exeter boys.

He glances down at me. 'How you doing, Novak?'

'I'm good.' I really am. I've even forgiven him for goading the others into the whole me-and-Nate thing. 'How about you, Conway?'

'I am absolutely flying,' he says, just as another Party Boat girl passes with a tray of shots. Zack bows to her before taking four in his massive hands. He offers me one, wedged between his pinky and ring finger, and I take it and down it. Someone must have just put a load more meat on the barbecue; I can smell the fat in the air, smoke drifting this way. I look over, feeling suddenly hungry. Zack notices straight away.

'Eatin's cheatin', Novak.'

I laugh. 'Oh, come on. Just one teensy drumstick?'

He laughs, pointing at a girl in front of us who's examining the yellowish, stringy piece of chicken on her paper plate. There are a *lot* of veins in it. 'Well, if you think a dose of food poisoning is exactly what your holiday's missing, Hope-Dogg . . .'

'Yeah.' I look away from the gross chicken. 'Maybe I'm all right after all.'

'That's my girl.' Zack passes me another shot and necks one too. 'Hey, who are your mates?'

I glance in the direction he's looking. Ness and Emily are posing as Hayley takes a picture.

'Oh, they're nice,' I say. 'They've just finished A levels.'

He's still looking at them – at Emily in particular. 'Introduce me?' he asks.

'Yeah,' Dev says, draping an arm round me and leaning his head on my shoulder. 'Introduce us to your lovely new friends, Hopey.'

Ness looks up then, and waves. So I gesture for them to come over, and introduce everyone just as the siren sounds beside the keg.

'Oh God, another game,' Hayley says, handing me the bottle of melon stuff, which has a couple of inches left in it. 'I'm already smashed.'

I laugh. 'At least you're getting your money's worth.'

'Good point.'

We head after the others, who are making their way further down the beach, where the Party Boat people are picking volunteers. Zack volunteers himself and Emily, who looks a bit unsure but goes along with it, laughing. Dev has his arm round Ness now, chatting away though it doesn't look like he's making a whole lot of sense.

'Your mates seem nice,' Hayley says.

'Yeah, they're cool,' I say, suddenly registering that Logan and Nate aren't with us – I haven't seen either of them since we got here.

'Right!' one of the Party Boat girls yells, hands cupped round her mouth. 'It's time for the sex-positions game!'

There's a round of whooping and cheering. Hayley rolls her eyes. Zack waggles his eyebrows at Emily, who laughs.

'You all know how it works,' the girl continues. 'The couple who can get in the most positions in sixty-nine seconds –' there's a fresh chorus of cheers at that – 'will win a go on the keg of dreams. Couples, are you ready?'

There are four other couples, apart from Zack and Emily, each with their own Party Boat rep to count their positions. They all give the thumbs-up, and the girl blows her whistle for the game to begin.

It's not very sexy – they all look ridiculous, moving from standing to lying to sitting on each other, legs thrown up and bent back and grabbed. I watch as Zack turns Emily onto her hands and knees and then drags her up to standing, picks her up. She's sort of going along with it but you can tell from her face that she'd rather be literally anywhere else than right here at this particular moment in time. Even unflappable Zack seems suitably embarrassed, though he doesn't exactly look like he's not enjoying it. Beside me, Ness has her phone up in the air, filming the whole thing.

Zack and Emily don't win – there's another couple who look like they're actually on fast-forward, they flip through positions so fast. When the second whistle blows, and the reps announce the scores, those two are like ten ahead of everyone else. They high-five each other and Zack shrugs at Emily, like *What can you do?*

The winning couple – a girl with a platinum-blonde bob and one of the stag-party guys from earlier – step forward to claim their prize. 'Kind of glad Em didn't win,' Hayley says. 'This looks like it's going to get messy really fast.'

I nod. The guy is being held in a handstand by two of the reps, while another holds a funnel in his mouth. The girl with the whistle is holding a hose, one end attached to the keg as she raises the other over the funnel. She gestures to the crowd and everyone around me obliges.

'Drink . . . drink . . . drink . . .'

Beer gushes into the funnel and we watch the rugby guy's Adam's apple bob madly up and down as he tries to swallow it upside down. He looks so ridiculous I can't help laughing. Zack and Emily definitely got off lightly here. Blonde bob girl looks like she's wishing they hadn't been

71

quite so good at the game after all.

'Come on,' Ness says, still half supporting a grinning Dev. 'Let's go get a drink. To drink standing the right way up.'

WE SIT NEAR the edge of the water, Dev and Ness sharing a cigarette, Zack and Hayley arguing about politics. Emily is telling me about her boyfriend back home while we work our way through another round of beers.

'He wouldn't care about the game,' she says. 'He's not the jealous type. If anything, he's a bit *too* laid back.'

'Is that even a thing?'

She laughs. 'I guess not. I just worry that when we both go off to uni, we'll drift apart. Like, he's not the type to text every five minutes. When he's on Football Manager, I think he actually forgets that anyone outside the game exists.'

I laugh and offer her a shot from the tray that Ness has managed to steal from the bar. Well, it's not actually *stealing*, is it? We paid for the tickets. And none of us have eaten any of the chicken or the dodgy-looking kebabs also on offer. We're definitely owed a few extra drinks.

'Hey, I need a wee,' Emily says, glancing at the queue winding its way out of the little building. 'Will you come with me and stand guard if I go behind a tree?'

'Yeah, sure,' I say, standing up. Wow, I'm drunker than I thought, my legs wobbly on the sand. I've no idea how long we've been sitting there because the sun is starting to dip back down towards the sea, the sky already turning pink.

Feeling a bit disorientated, I follow Emily into the woods, hunting for a suitably private spot. That actually turns out to be harder than expected – even though we're technically all supposed to be keeping the party strictly to the beach, there are loads of people back here. A group huddled round what definitely smells like a spliff, and then two girls crouched over by another tree, heads bowed together over something I can't see. There's a couple kissing – like, really kissing – up against a tree, and in the distance I can see another pair who aren't as hidden as they think they are, her shorts being slid down.

'Err . . . How about over here?' Emily's found a wilting, spiky bush which, once you're on the right side of it, offers a quite nice view of the sea. 'OK, all clear?'

I look around, but it seems like we're mostly out of sight and no one's heading our way. 'All clear.'

'Great.' She slides down her shorts and hitches her kaftan out of the way. 'Because I am *busting*.'

'So you guys are flying back on Monday?' I ask, mostly to cover the sound of her wee hitting the dirt.

'Yeah.' Emily sighs. 'And then the next thing to look forward to is results day, aka Shit Gets Real Day.'

I put a hand out to steady myself on a tree. I really am quite drunk now. 'What did you say you had planned for next year?' I can't remember if she's told me already but hopefully she won't either.

'Psychology,' she says, standing and sliding her shorts back up. 'Well, that's the plan anyway. I honestly don't know what's going to happen with results. I need three As to get my first choice.'

'Oh wow.'

'Yeah.' She picks her way back round the bush. 'Anyway, let's not think about that now. Do you need the loo?'

Now she mentions it, I really do. A lot of beers and melon-flavoured green stuff have congregated in my bladder, and now I'm standing up, it's pretty hard to ignore. So I shift round the bush, avoiding Emily's puddle, and crouch down with my dress hitched up.

'Incoming,' she says, just as I finish, and I stand up and see Logan and Nate walking through the trees.

'Oh, I know them,' I say, waving to get their attention. Nate sees me and nudges Logan, diverting them in our direction, but I can't help noticing that neither of them look like they're having a very good time. Nate's face is serious, and Logan's still choosing to look anywhere but at me.

'Guys, this is Emily,' I say, when they get up close to us. 'We've been hanging out with her and her friends on the beach.' I look at them carefully again. *Where have you been?* I want to add.

'Hey,' Nate says, shaking Emily's hand. 'Nate – Logan.'

'How's it going?' Logan asks, and just like that, they're normal again. I wonder if I imagined the atmosphere before.

Emily smiles at him. 'You guys having fun? You all look soberer than your friend Dev at least.'

Nate groans. 'Is he off his face?'

'Yep.' I lean against a tree. 'He's in love with the whole world.'

'So what's new?' Logan jokes, and when I catch his eye, he smiles at me.

'What about Zack?' Nate asks.

75

Emily shrugs. 'He seems fine. If a bit . . . grabby. And kind of . . . big on opinion-having.'

Nate and Logan both laugh. 'Yeah, sounds about right,' Nate says, his eyes lingering on Emily.

'Shall we head back?' I ask. The sun's sinking lower and the shadows in the woods are stretching out. 'It'll be dark soon.'

We start to walk back towards the beach and the others, and I wonder again where Nate and Logan have been all this time. Logan stumbles as we walk, and although Emily's right – they definitely *are* soberer than Dev (not exactly difficult) – I know them both well enough to tell that they're definitely still feeling the effects of the ouzo.

'I think they're going to play another game in a bit,' Emily says. 'Not that anyone's really up for it after the last one – whoa!' Her sandal catches on the edge of a tree root and she trips, but Nate's reflexes are clearly working fine despite the booze because he catches her arm.

'Easy.'

She blushes and smiles at him. 'Thanks. God, I'm really drunk.'

'No problem.' He stays walking next to her, leaving me and Logan a couple of steps behind. I glance up at him.

'Are you having a good day?'

He nods. 'You?'

'Yeah, it's great –'

'Wa-heeeeey!' Some guy comes crashing out of the bushes to our left, grinning at us. 'What a fucking day, am I right?'

He pulls his sunglasses off to grin at us, and he looks

completely out of it. His eyes are sort of glazed and his jaw grinds but he just carries on grinning, his head bobbing to the beat from the beach. He's wearing a baggy vest top, the straps stretched and thin, so that when he moves his nipple pokes out of one side, and shorts that are just a bit too tight, giving us all a reasonable idea of his . . . well, you know.

'Yeah, it's great, mate,' Nate says, moving to step round him. 'Let's get back on it, shall we?'

But the guy stares at him, his teeth clenching and unclenching. 'Just tryna be friendly.' His eyes bob from Nate to Logan and then focus on me. 'Hey, honey.'

I roll my eyes. 'Come on, let's go.'

'Don't be such a bitch,' the guy says, but he's already bored, already moving on to Emily. 'You're not a bitch, are you? You're too pretty to be a bitch.'

Emily pushes past him. 'I prefer guys in control of their faces, generally,' she says, and the guy laughs hysterically, like she's made the best joke he's ever heard, and starts stumbling off the way we've just come.

But as he passes me and Logan, he stops. He looks Logan in the eye and shakes his head, really slow. 'What's a fit girl like her doing with you?' he asks. And as he trips his way off, I swear I hear him mutter a word under his breath.

I stop and spin on my heel immediately, my drunkenness evaporating. 'What the f—'

'Hope.' Logan grabs my arm. 'Don't bother. He's a mess, it's not worth it.'

'He just called you a –'

He shrugs. His hand is still round my arm and we both look

at it until he lets go. 'Come on,' he says. Nate and Emily have stopped up ahead and are looking back at us, confused. 'We're having a good time,' Logan says. 'Forget it.'

And so I follow him and the others out of the woods. But the whole time I can hear that stupid guy laughing.

THE AIR STARTS to get cooler, the sky turning inky. If you thought things might be getting mellower, you'd be wrong.

The Party Boat reps have lit torches around the edge of the beach and turned on UV lights above the DJ. Their super-soakers are filled with glow paint now, and we all press closer to the stage, desperate to get into their line of fire. We're all sweaty and splashed with neon, dancing to some track we've never heard. I'm bouncing against Nate, JB, Logan, all of them with their T-shirts off, the paint on their chests coming off on my face and dress. We're all out of breath with singing and laughing, and everything is amazing.

By the time I step away, my feet aching, the sky is properly dark. In the circle of light – at least one person has already stumbled into a torch, burning their arm – we feel like a warm little bubble, like there's nothing else around us. But I can make out people outside the flickering light, people sitting and standing in the shadows, chilling out on the dark bit of the beach. I find a bucket full of ice and bottled water and grab one, drinking half of it down.

'Hope!' I glance round and see Ness and Hayley waving at me. They've found a big chunk of driftwood to sit on, just close enough to one of the torches to make it feel a bit like a campfire. I go over, taking my flip-flops off and sticking them under my arm. The sand feels cool and wet under my feet.

'I can't dance any more,' Hayley says. 'I'll spew.'

I offer her my water and we watch everyone else dancing for a while. There's a couple a little further down the beach from us, lying on the sand. They're kissing, her leg over his, and Ness rolls her eyes. 'Get a room.'

'Where's Emily?' I ask, and Hayley looks around.

'She went to get a drink,' she says. 'Hmm . . . Oh, wait, there she is!' She frowns into the dark. 'Hang on, isn't that your mate?'

I follow her gaze and see Emily heading towards us, Zack beside her. She's saying something, her hands flying wildly about as she tells a story, and Zack's laughing, his head bent towards hers. They step round two girls sprawled, laughing, on the sand and Zack puts his hand on Emily's back, pulling her closer to him.

'Yeah,' I say. 'I don't think he knows she's got a boyfriend.'

'Hope!' I turn at the sound of my name again, and see Nate heading over, pulling his T-shirt back on. 'This has got to be the sickest party I've ever been to,' he says, sinking down next to me and taking the water Hayley offers him.

I smile at him. I feel drunk but in the nicest, comfiest way. I feel warm inside and like I just want to sit here, with these people, forever.

'Hey, guys.' Emily and Zack have reached us, and I notice she's moved away from him.

'Novak, you look wasted,' Zack says, laughing. 'You too, Nate-Dogg.'

80

'I'm not!' I say, but I wobble in my seat, and that makes me laugh. 'Yeah, OK, maybe a bit.'

'I totally forgot to get a drink,' Emily says, laughing too. 'I think it's me who's wasted.'

'We'll go,' Zack says, winking at her. 'Won't we, Nate?'

Nate shrugs. 'I could go for another beer.'

He doesn't really look like he needs it, but hey, it's a party. Zack looks at the rest of us. 'Girls? Drink?'

'Yeah, I reckon I can handle another cocktail,' Hayley says, already perked up.

'Yup, me too,' Ness leans back, looking up at the sky. 'If you're sure you don't mind.'

'I'll help,' I say, because I can't see Nate making it back across the beach without spilling most of the drinks. Although, standing up, I can't really see myself helping all that much, either.

'Team player, Novak,' Zack says, slinging an arm round my shoulders. I can smell the booze coming off him in waves. 'I've always said it.'

The bar is looking pretty low on stock, with all of the premade cocktails gone and just bottles of beer swishing round in melted ice left. But Zack leans across and says something to the girl in the Party Boat T-shirt – at first she shakes her head at him, but he keeps talking, that Zack Conway grin on his face, and slowly but surely she starts to smile too. Before we know it, she's pulling a bottle of something out from under the makeshift bar, pouring three huge shots for us.

I think that's where it all starts to go really wrong.

* * *

The warm feeling spreads through me and I go back to dance with Logan and Dev, leaving Nate and Zack with the girls. Everyone's faces blur together in the firelight, and the music thuds through me and at first I don't recognise the girls I see with Logan and Dev.

Dev comes close to me, his eyes still big and rolling. He's shouting something but I can't make it out. Someone brushes against me, their skin warm and wet.

'*From the hotel,*' Dev is saying. '*Rachel. Lucy.*'

When I realise it's the girls from the coach, from the first day, I throw my arms around them like they're my best friends.

We dance and dance and the moon comes up in the sky, big and yellow.

'It looks like cheese,' I say to Logan, and when I hear it out loud I realise how funny that is.

'Cheese!' I say to Dev, to Lucy. I point. 'It looks like *cheese.*'

We all laugh. We keep dancing.

The music cuts out and everyone is sad. The chant starts somewhere near the front and swells back like a wave we all catch.

'*One. More. Song. One. More. Song.*'

The DJ shakes his head at us. He is not with the wave.

A Party Boat rep picks me up from the sand. 'Time to go,' he says, and I pout at him. 'There's cocktails on board,' he says, and when I skip in the direction of the boat, he pats me on the bum. I link my arm through Logan's and we join the queue.

'Is it late?' I ask. 'It feels late.'

'It's just the start,' Logan says, and he laughs.

The queue is long and the people in it don't really want to get on the boat at all.

'Hey, that's Nate,' Logan says, and I look up and see the crowd in front of us moving, pushing. People are shouting.

Logan tugs me forward and then Rachel is there, a hand over her mouth. 'That guy is a dick,' she says, and I tell her no, but then I see where she is looking.

The guy in the vest top from the woods before is pushed up close to Nate, getting right in his face. He's saying something but it's dark and people are pushing and I can't see.

'Oi!' Zack's voice is loud enough for everyone to hear. He puts a hand on the guy's shoulder, pulls him away. 'Leave it out, yeah? Everyone's having a good time, no need, eh?'

The guy looks at him. 'Fuck you,' he says, and he shoves Zack, hard, so that Zack stumbles into Rachel and me. People around us laugh and the guy is gone.

The queue starts to move again and I tell everyone who will listen that there shouldn't be fighting. There's no need for fighting.

We're all having a good time.

WE'RE BACK ON the boat, its lights flickering across the black water. The stars are out and the moon is big and yellow and cheese. Everyone is my friend and I have so much to say. I dance with the stag party and I wander around the deck, saying things to people and looking up at the stars and the big yellow moon. The music pulses through my feet and a breeze drifts in from the water and lifts my hair from my face. I can't stop smiling.

I'm downstairs, sitting in a cosy little knot with my boys again, with my boys and with Ness, all of us slumped on beanbags and playing Twenty-One, which is supposed to be the easiest drinking game of all but somehow all the numbers are getting muddled up in my head and I keep saying the wrong one or speaking when it's not my turn and I can't stop laughing and everyone else is laughing too and I have to drink, drink, drink. I rest my head on JB's shoulder and he smells of aftershave and barbecue and ouzo and everything feels so nice.

Time jumps again and I'm back up on the deck, with a drink I don't remember getting. I'm on the other side of the boat to the dance floor and it's quiet here, no flashing disco lights or

Party Boat reps with water guns. There are two boys leaning over the railing, but they're too far away and it's too dark for me to make out their faces. One of them is being sick over the side while the other rubs his back. I want to help but I can't seem to make my legs do what I want them to, and before I can, they're gone.

I am dancing, whirling, my glass is empty but people offer me theirs, people pour bottles into my open mouth. I spin round and round and the lights hit their eyes as they watch me. Hands touch mine and touch me and everyone is laughing, I'm laughing. The beach gets closer and closer.

'IS SHE OK?'

I turn onto my side, trying to burrow back into sleep. I'm dreaming that I'm walking across a bog, my feet sinking. I don't know why but I know I need to get to a ruined cottage on the other side. The bog is full of weeds, but when I look down I see they're hands, pale and grey, stretching out of the mud with their fingers curling.

But one is attached to me. Its fingers lock on me and I know it's going to drag me down with it, suck me into the ground.

'Hello? You all right, mate?'

Hang on.

The voice is not a dream.

The hand on my shoulder, gently shaking me, is not a dream.

It all comes to me gradually; the sun on my skin, the sand underneath me. The pain in my head. The slow, horrible wave of dread rising up inside me.

I open my eyes.

I'm on the beach.

The weirdest thing is that at first I feel relieved. I'm just on the beach, I've just fallen asleep. That's embarrassing but it's OK.

But then, my stomach dropping, I take in the fact that

it's daytime, not night – and that there are two guys I don't recognise leaning over me.

And my dress is up around my waist.

I sit up, scrambling to cover myself. The two guys back off immediately, their eyes wide and concerned. They're a bit older than me, but not much, both of them in swimming shorts, one with a cap on and the other with long, shaggy hair.

'You all right, mate?' the one with the cap says again. Scouse.

'Bit of a heavy night?' the other one asks, offering me a bottle of water.

I look around, frantically trying to piece everything together. *We were on the boat. We were on the boat. Then what?*

'What time is it?' I ask, my voice coming out all scratchy and slurred.

'Nine, mate. Do you want us to walk you somewhere? Where you staying?'

Where are my friends?

I feel terrible, my stomach churning, the first scrabbles of panic in my chest. 'I'm OK,' I say, standing up and wobbling. *Where's my bag?*

'This yours?' The guy with the cap picks up my little blue handbag, brushing the sand off it. It's all squashed; I must have slept on it.

'Thanks.' I take it and I notice that my hands are shaking. I still feel drunk; hammered really. Nothing seems real.

My phone is still in my bag but the battery's dead. There's a creased-up receipt but no sign of any of the euro notes I remember putting in there. I look around again. There's the boat, docked where it was yesterday, the shutters on the ticket office being pushed up by a guy in Hawaiian shorts. On the deck, someone else is mopping. The boat shines in the sun.

Where are my friends?

'Seriously, you OK?' The boys are still standing in front of me, looking at me. 'You want some money for a cab or something?'

I need to get away from here. I need to get away from these feelings, this panic. I need to be back with my boys, for this to be over and done and just a thing we can all laugh about round the pool.

'I'm all right,' I say, because if I say it out loud, if I say it enough, it'll surely be true. I turn around before they can say anything else. I walk as confidently as I can towards the road, but my legs are wobbly and the toe post of one of my flip-flops has worked itself loose, the strap baggy and too big to hold my foot.

I make it to the edge of the beach, a patch of spiky bushes with bottles and plastic bags marooned between their fronds, before I throw up.

WHEN I GET back to the hotel, the building swims in front of me. My stomach feels empty and raw and everything seems distant, like I'm watching myself walk towards the automatic doors in a film or a computer game. Nothing seems real apart from the feeling that I might be sick again.

I shuffle past the reception desk, my broken flip-flop clacking against the tiles. The cleaner has just bleached the floor and the smell burns the back of my throat. I feel like the receptionists are looking at me funny.

They must see people in some pretty awful states round here. But they're looking at me.

The first time I get a glimpse of myself is in the lift, its fingerprinted metal walls and the big mirror at the back reflecting my face, over and over. My eyes are wide and intense, make-up smudged under them but mostly dissolved – sweat and sea spray from the boat, the hours wiping it all away. I'm pale but also sunburnt, random patches of red blotchy against the rest of my sickly, sweaty skin.

All of this is far away.

All of this is just background noise while somewhere inside my head is a voice I can't shut up: *What happened?*

What happened what happened what happened

I'm not ready to answer that voice, not ready to realise that

I don't *have* the answers, and so I keep looking at my face. I look at the sunburn around my hairline, the sticky patch of something matted near one ear. I look down at my hands and see the torn nail, the usual night-out mystery crud underneath the others, the stamp from the boat fading on the inside of my wrist. I wait for the lift to ping.

The doors slide open on the third floor and the bleach smell is still there. I am still here.

My flip-flop finally gives out halfway up the corridor, the strap popping free. Sole left behind. I scoop it up and carry it the rest of the way. There's a fresh stain on the wall outside our apartment; a brownish spray near the floor. Someone dropped a kebab or a burger, I guess, sauce and grease splashing up. The food, whatever it was, has been removed by the cleaners but the marks are still there. Something to remember us by.

I feel in my bag again, afraid that I imagined it the first time. But no, my key, with its little plastic tag, is still there, jangling around with a lone euro. I slot it into the door and, for a minute, I just stand there.

Then I hear someone laughing inside.

And I remember.

I remember that I just woke up on my own on the beach and I am *angry*.

Angry feels a lot better.

I storm into the apartment, barely registering that Dev, Logan and Zack are sitting in the main room. I let the rage take over. I let it spill out and splatter.

'What. The. Fuck, you guys? *Where* the fuck were you?'

Dev, who looks like he was about to laugh when I came in,

and is still not sure whether he should, gapes at me. Logan looks bewildered.

But Zack? Zack just jumps right in.

'Here she is, boys,' he says, grinning at me. 'Look what the cat dragged in, eh? Who was the lucky boy, Hopey? You were a *right* handful last night.'

I stare at him, too sick to process his words properly. 'You left me,' I say. 'You all left me.'

Logan stands up. 'Left you where?'

'I don't know!' I can't breathe. I can't breathe. Breathe. Breathe.

'I woke up on the beach,' I say, trying to keep my voice normal and low. 'And none of you were there. I can't –' I'm too afraid to admit what I *can't*; what is still missing.

'Shit, Hope, you OK?' Dev comes towards me, a T-shirt flung over his bare shoulder, shorts chilli-sauce-stained. 'I'm sorry, I was messed up.'

'You guys left me,' I say again, without meaning to. It's all I can say. I say it again because anger felt better and I'm scared of feeling scared. 'You *left* me. What the hell?'

'What's your problem, Hope?' Zack says, both hands held palm out, like *Whoa whoa. Relax.* 'You're on a lads' holiday, you want to be one of the lads. We're not gonna babysit you.'

I stare at him. My stomach twists and dips and all I can think about is that boy shaking me awake. The way I sat up and expected it all to still be there: the boat, the music. My friends.

'You left me,' I say, because those are the only words I have. And then I turn and walk away.

I slam into the bedroom, yanking the flimsy door closed

behind me. I still can't quite catch my breath and fear is flickering in my chest, tiny wings beating against my ribs. I sit down on the bed, the thin sheet still rumpled from where one of the boys slept in it last night. They noticed my bed was empty but only for long enough to steal it. My head is pounding, an actual pulsing pain at my temples, and my mouth is sour and dry. I take another mental inventory of my body. Feet dirty, a small cut from my flip-flops between my toes, but otherwise OK. A bruise on my shin and a sticky splash mark on one calf which I hope is some kind of cocktail and not puke this time.

I feel like heaving again. Up, up, up. My thighs feel stiff, maybe, but that could be from the dancing?

The hem of my dress is a little torn. I try not to think of the way it had ridden up, right up, over my hip, when I woke up on the beach.

There's a knock on the door; gentle, three little taps.

When I don't respond, it creaks open a little.

'Hope?' Logan. He pokes his head into the room. 'Can I come in?'

I shrug. I still don't have the words.

He comes in and sinks down onto the edge of the other bed, where the pillow has a yellow dribble stain on it. What looks like ketchup is smudged across the sheet. He leans forward, resting his elbows near his knees, and looks at me. 'I'm really sorry about last night,' he says. 'I was wasted. No way I'd have gone home if I'd known you weren't with the others.'

I try to swallow but my throat feels sore. I still don't feel like I'm getting quite enough air.

'It's OK,' I hear myself saying. 'Everyone was a mess.'

'It's not all right,' he says, frowning. 'We're your mates. We should've been looking out for you.'

I have to turn away because the tightness in my chest, the fluttering panic, has solidified into a terrible pressure, a pressure I'm suddenly sure is tears.

'You OK?'

I pick up one of my T-shirts from the floor, fold it and then, not really sure where to put it, I just hold it and look out of the window at the pool below.

'Hope, your arm's bleeding.'

I glance down and notice that my hands are still shaking, just a little bit. I need to eat something. Drink some water. Lie down maybe.

I stand there, still staring at my arms.

What happened what happened what happened

'Here.' He stands up and comes closer, tentative like I'm a tiger in a zoo. 'Your elbow, see?'

I turn my arm, see a smear of drying red, sand stuck in it like glitter.

'You should wash it,' Logan says, reaching out as if he might touch me. He seems to change his mind when he sees my face.

'It's fine,' I say. I drop the folded T-shirt into my case and turn away again. 'So what's going on today?'

'Hope.'

I can't. I can't look at him.

'Did something happen?'

I pick up a towel from the wooden chair by the window. 'God, I feel like shit,' I say. 'I'm gonna get in the shower.'

I can't look at him.

You might think that I still want to remember. That I lie awake at night and try and try to conjure those missing pieces. That word you whispered or the moment your hand closed around my arm.

But I don't. Not any more. Those memories can just be yours.
You can keep them safe.
You can let them fester.

LOGAN

I'LL NEVER FORGET the way she looked that day. The way she looked at all of us. The way, when it was just the two of us alone in that room, she couldn't look at me.

When she said she wanted to have a shower, I just nodded.

God, I'm ashamed of that now.

When I went back into the living room, the others were quiet. Except for Zack, who was acting like nothing was wrong – and doing it loudly.

'Right, it's our last night, boys,' he was saying, boiling the kettle but then checking the fridge and taking out beers. 'What's everyone want to do?'

'Who was with her last?' Nate asked, ignoring Zack. 'JB?'

JB shook his head. 'I . . . I wasn't with any of you. I was chatting to some people and couldn't find you so I went to the strip with them. I thought maybe I'd bump into you lot there.'

'I was with her for a bit,' Dev said. He was looking down at his hands, like he didn't want to meet anyone's eyes. 'Me and Ness, we got off the boat with her. But I'd left my phone in that beanbag bit so I went back on to get it – and then I went home with Lucy.' He looked up then and grinned.

'For fucksake,' Nate said. 'This doesn't make any sense. We were all right there. How did no one see her?'

'Oh, bore off,' Zack said, putting beers down on the table. 'You couldn't see six fucking inches in front of your face last night, Nate-Dogg. This isn't some kind of murder mystery. Hope got absolutely twatted and fell asleep on the beach. Boo-hoo. Why are we even still talking about it?'

I didn't say anything.

And yes, I'm ashamed of that now too.

WHEN HOPE CAME out of the bathroom, she went into the bedroom without saying anything – without even glancing in our direction. I wanted to go in there again. But also I didn't.

Dev glanced at his phone and then stood up. 'I'm going to meet Lucy,' he said.

Zack gave him a wolf-howl, which was exactly what he wanted.

'You guys can come if you want,' Dev said. 'We're going for food down the Red Lion – you know that place at the end of the strip? They're showing the new Jack Reacher this afternoon, rooftop cinema thing.' He glanced at me and then at the closed bedroom door. 'I mean, if you want to.'

'Nah, you go,' Zack said, even though I could tell everyone was thinking it was tempting. 'We won't crash your date, Dev-Dogg. You gotta meet us later though – last night on tour!'

Dev nodded and then left. The bedroom was still silent.

'Well, we'll go down the pool after these,' Zack said, looking at his beer. He was the only one who'd started drinking his. 'No point sitting around in here all day, eh?'

He stared at me hard until I took a sip of mine. The fridge was broken and it was warm and tasted metallic in my mouth, like blood. I put it back down on the table.

JB glanced at the bedroom door. 'Maybe I should . . .'

But before he could finish his sentence, the door opened and Hope came out in shorts and a T-shirt, her wet hair combed back from her face.

'Beer, Novak?' Zack asked her. 'Hair of the dog?'

I expected her to tell him where to go. But she just took the beer and sat down.

'Thought we'd go down to the pool after this,' Zack said.

Hope took a swig of her beer. 'Cool.'

'Hope, we're really sorry –' Nate started, but Hope just cut him off.

'It's fine.' She took another, longer drink of her beer. She'd cleaned the sand from the graze on her arm and there was a plaster on one of her feet too. 'So, what's the plan for tonight?'

Nate looked at me, and I looked at Hope again. I knew her pretty well by that point – I knew the way her voice sounded when she was happy, when she was angry. When she was sad. And I knew the way she sounded when she was trying to avoid a conversation.

'We've gotta hit the strip hard,' Zack said. 'Give them something to remember us by, right?'

Hope laughed. 'Yeah, OK then.'

'Hope, are you sure you're all right?' JB asked.

'Course she is,' Zack said, draining the rest of his beer. 'Hardly the first time you've got so hammered you can't remember what you've got up to or who's been in you, is it, Novak?'

And just like that, Hope got up and left, the apartment door slamming behind her. JB looked at the three of us, shaking his head, and then followed her. In the silence he left behind, we could hear him calling her name.

'Fucksake,' Nate said, standing up. 'I can't deal with this. I'm going to find Dev.'

The door slammed for a third time and then it was just me and Zack. I stared at him.

'You can't say anything,' he said with a shrug.

'They're going to wonder where we were,' I said. 'They're going to start asking questions.'

His eyes narrowed. 'You can't say *anything*,' he said again. 'And you know exactly why not.'

IT WASN'T EXACTLY the last night of the holiday any of us had imagined. Zack and I went to find Dev and Nate at the Red Lion, with Hope and JB nowhere to be seen. We ate burgers and drank beer and my mouth was dry and tasted like dust.

Lucy was obviously disappointed with us.

'You guys were way more fun last night,' she said.

'Exactly!' Zack put his arm round her. 'You're my kind of girl, Lucy. Shall we get the shots in?'

'Yeah, all right.' She hopped off her bar stool and followed him. Dev watched them miserably.

'You reckon Hope and JB will come meet us?' he asked, picking at the edge of the table. I could see that Nate was watching him. When Dev glanced up, Nate just shrugged and then looked away.

Lucy came back with a tray of tequilas. 'So bored of all the apple-flavoured sugary shit,' she said, shrugging. 'Time to get serious, I say.'

Behind her back, Zack pressed a hand to his heart and mimed fainting. She wasn't actually his kind of girl though – the only girlfriends he ever had were model-beautiful and snobby and preferred to stay at home with their friends while he was out with the lads. *That* was his type of girl.

'Here you go,' Lucy said, handing me a shot. 'Hey, what happened to your hands?'

'Oh nothing,' I said, taking my glass and trying to resist hiding them under the table. 'I just fell into a wall walking home last night. Pissed up.'

It was only a cut, a puffy knuckle. Hardly even noticeable – but she'd noticed.

'Clumsy,' Nate said, his voice even, his eyes locked on mine. It was me who looked away first.

'Right, shots!' Zack said, sliding a saucer of manky lemon wedges and a salt-shaker into the middle of the table. We all loaded ourselves up, and then downed our tequilas.

I was starting to feel like I needed it.

We ended up in Rodeo again. Rachel and a couple of people from the boat met us there, and by 10 p.m. everyone was drunk again. I drank and I talked and I even danced when Rachel and another girl pulled me onto the floor with them.

I tried to keep a smile on my face. I've had a lot of practice at that.

JB texted to say that he and Hope were having dinner and that they'd probably join us later. I wasn't exactly holding my breath.

Whenever Zack got near me, he kept patting me on the back, offering to buy me drinks. 'Enjoy yourself, buddy,' he kept saying. 'Forget about last night, mate.' And I tried. I tried to take his drinks and tried to stop myself thinking about the boat, about that beach. About Hope flopping round the deck, starry-eyed and trusting everyone. Laughing her head off. Looking up at the stars.

Later, I was about to walk into the gents' when I heard Zack and Dev standing at the urinals.

'Listen,' Zack was saying. 'I don't get what the big deal is. You want to play with the big boys, you've got to be up to the game. If Hope couldn't handle it, she should've stayed at home. Nobody forced all those drinks on her, did they? You've gotta know your limits – you can't just expect everyone else to pick up the pieces when you've got too messed up to look after yourself.'

I let the door click closed. I had to go and stand outside and breathe for a while. I thought about the time Zack's brother made him do three dirty pints on his birthday and Nate and I carried him home. I thought about the time I drank a bottle of grappa my auntie bought back from holiday and Hope stayed up all night because she was afraid I'd choke on my own vomit.

I went back inside. I drank more.

JB and Hope never came to meet us. Like I say, I wasn't surprised. By the end of the night, Dev was getting off with Lucy again, and Zack was doing Jägerbombs with the rest of the girls.

I was leaning against the railings outside, thinking about just going home in the hope that the others would be back there already, when Nate came out.

'Shame they didn't come,' he said.

'Yeah.'

'She's right to be angry. We were out of order.'

I nodded but I didn't look at him. I *couldn't* look at him.

'She was fucked up,' Nate said. 'You saw her on that boat.'

I nodded. 'I know. I *know*, OK.'

'We shouldn't have left her there.'

'Well, *you* left all of us,' I said, because there was panic in my chest and I couldn't stand it. 'What even happened to you, anyway?'

I knew he didn't know. I knew he didn't remember. I'd seen the state of him as he went staggering off towards the strip. We shouldn't have left him either. But we did.

'I don't fucking know, all right?' Nate said. 'That's not the point. We're all friends and we're supposed to look out for each other. So why weren't any of us looking out for Hope?'

THE APARTMENT WAS dark when we got back, and the door to JB and Hope's room was closed.

'Anyone for a beer?' Zack asked hopefully, and because none of us said no, he went to the kitchen and took out four.

The others sat down but I went out to the balcony and looked down at the empty pool. Without Lucy and the others around, the atmosphere between us all felt tense and weird. I'd been expecting Dev to go home with Lucy again – I got the feeling he had too – but when we'd left the club he'd come with us, muttering something about having to get up for the flight in the morning. I assumed she'd blown him off and he was just trying to save face and, unusually, no one ribbed him for it.

My insides twisted every time I thought about the night before. I put my hands on the balcony railing and focused on looking down at the water, taking deep breaths. But my eyes kept returning to my scraped, swollen knuckles, and when I turned away and saw one of Hope's T-shirts hanging over the edge of the railing where she'd left it to dry, I had to turn around and go inside.

I went back in, hoping to think about something else, but Zack was sitting in one of the armchairs, feet up on the coffee table. 'I dunno what JB's got his knickers in a twist about anyway,' he said. 'Not like he was in a rush to take her home, was it? He buggered off with these mysterious new friends of his – and there's something a bit off with that story anyway.'

'Keep your voice down,' I said, willing him to shut up. I couldn't understand why he, of all people, would want to start picking at the threads of where we'd all been the night before.

Zack rolled his eyes at me, but he shrugged and shut up.

Nate had been quiet since he'd followed me out of Rodeo. He was drinking the beer Zack had given him fast, pulling it down in long swigs – when he noticed me watching him, it was me who looked away first.

'Can't believe Dev's the only one who got into a girl's bed,' Zack said, reaching over to chink his bottle against Dev's. 'Well in, mate. Not that it was all that difficult, huh? Lucy's a right goer.'

Nate put down his bottle, hard, on the coffee table and stood up. 'I'm gonna go to bed,' he said. 'Knackered.'

He went to the bathroom. Given that his bed was the sofa, that meant it was our cue to do the same, and I was glad. I went into our room and stripped to my pants, climbing under the sheet of the camp bed with my beer still in my hand.

Dev fell asleep almost straight away, one foot hanging over the edge of the bed, and Zack turned off the light as he came back from his turn in the bathroom, a towel round his neck. I took a sip of my beer and listened to him climb into bed next to Dev. I waited for him to say something, but there was just a shuffle as he turned onto his side, pulling the sheet up over him. And then his breathing got slower and longer until it started to turn into a snore.

I lay there in the dark, looking up at the ceiling and drinking my beer.

My bruised hand was starting to throb.

WE FLEW BACK to the UK the next day mostly in silence. Hope kept her headphones in for most of the coach journey and then she picked the window seat on the plane, with JB beside her and Nate on the other side of him. I was left to take the last of the seats in front, with Zack and Dev. It was Dev who was feeling sick this time after a dodgy kebab on the way home from Rodeo, and again nobody had the energy to tease him. He spent most of the time sleeping, and after a while I felt like maybe that was the easiest thing for me too.

I woke up as we were landing, my mouth dry and my neck cricked from sleeping in a weird position. The sky was grey and as the plane swooped down towards Stansted, I saw the flashing blue lights of three police cars racing along the motorway. I closed my eyes and kept them closed until the plane was parked at the gate and everyone had started taking their bags out of the overhead lockers.

Dev's parents had come to pick him, JB and Hope up, which left me and Nate to get a lift with Zack's dad. Zack's dad in his blinged-up Range Rover and his designer jeans. He'd pulled up in a 'No Parking' zone outside Arrivals and honked at us as soon as we stepped out onto the walkway.

At least that meant less time for awkward goodbyes.

'All right, boys!' Zack's dad, Gordon, said as we all climbed into the car. He had his hair slicked back and Radio 1 playing loud. 'You all look like shit.' He jerked his car out into the traffic, cutting up a taxi.

'Yeah thanks, Dad,' Zack said from the front seat. He was quieter than normal, and the tense journey had obviously bothered him too.

'Good holiday then?' Gordon asked, swinging out onto a roundabout and giving the middle finger to someone who honked their horn.

'Yeah,' we all said, unconvincingly.

'Go on then,' Gordon said. 'Who got the most pussy? Bet it was you, Nate, eh? Bet you had them all over ya.'

Nate shifted uncomfortably in his seat. 'Nah, Mr C.'

'Nope, not your kind of girl, I suppose,' Gordon said, picking up the can of Red Bull in the cup-holder and taking a swig. 'You like a classy lady, don't you, Nate? You've always been a man of taste. That – what was her name?'

'Polly,' Zack said.

'That's right. Pretty Polly. What happened to her? She was a – I shouldn't say this boys, but – she was an absolutely quality piece of ass, even at fifteen.'

'She moved to Australia,' Nate said, looking out of the window.

'That's right.' Another slurp of Red Bull, and then the can went back into the cup-holder. Gordon's attention turned to Zack. 'What about you, boyo? Get your willy wet?'

This time Nate snuck a look at me. I raised an eyebrow at him, knowing we were both thinking the same thing. My dad had plenty of faults – living a continent away, for one – but one thing he had going strongly in his favour was that he'd never asked me if I'd got my . . . well, you know.

Zack laughed. 'Spoilt for choice, Dad. They were throwing themselves at us, weren't they, guys?'

That's not exactly how I'd describe it, but I felt a bit sorry for him in front of his dad, so I just murmured something that could have been a yes.

'Yeah, well, you don't want the ones who are gagging for it, that's what you always forget,' Gordon said, overtaking a lorry. 'No sport in that, son.'

I turned on my phone – I'd forgotten to after the flight. It buzzed with a message from Mum asking what time I'd be back, and then a Snapchat from my cousin Steph – her face with a zombie filter applied to it ('Got ma hair did') – but that was it. I thought about messaging the others, asking how the journey was going or saying how good the holiday had been or maybe just coming right out and saying how shit it was that things were weird between all of us.

But I didn't.

The twisting, anxious feeling in my gut got worse.

At home that night, I lay on my bed watching some crap comedy on TV and looking through Instagram. I hadn't had enough data to upload anything over the holiday, but JB had posted loads of stuff, and Dev was obviously going on a spree now he was back home. About a million selfies of him in his neon sunglasses, with various new friends in various bars. I scrolled through them, and saw one JB had posted yesterday, of him and Hope having dinner. He'd obviously asked the waiter or someone to take it as they were both in shot, sitting at a table absolutely covered with food.

He'd captioned it:

```
Last night dinner with ma girl @hopemnovak
#fatties #malia2017 #ontour #whatababe
```

Hope was smiling, a loaded fork in her hand, a glass of wine in front of her. At least they'd had a good night. That made me happy.

My phone started ringing, the picture disappearing to show the caller ID. Zack. My heart sank.

'Zack?'

'Yo.'

'All right?'

I could hear a door closing on Zack's side of the phone, the noise of a TV getting quieter. 'Look, mate, I just wanted to talk about the other night. I can tell it's bothering you.'

I didn't say anything. I didn't trust myself to.

'Loges, it's really not a big deal. Just, you know, boys will be boys. I'm sure the kid was fine.'

When I still didn't say anything, he changed tack.

'He had it coming, Logan. You know it.'

When I couldn't stay silent any longer, my voice didn't sound like my own. 'I don't want to talk about this, Zack.'

'Sure you don't, mate. But I just want you to stop beating yourself up about it. You did what you had to do, we both did. And I've checked online, there's nothing about it. No requests for witnesses, no mention anywhere. We're all good.'

All good. Yeah, right. But I did feel relieved, I'll admit. Of course I did.

'I've gotta go,' I said.

'Yeah, OK, mate. See you round Nate's on Friday though, right?'

'Yep,' I said, because it was easiest. That's a thing I do. I'm not proud of that either.

After Zack hung up, I turned the TV off. I wanted to believe him that nothing was going to happen, no consequences. I hadn't dared google it myself – I'd spent the whole of the flight expecting police to be waiting for us at the airport, and then the whole of the drive back expecting them to be outside my house. I knew it was stupid, but my brain's good at imagining stuff like that. It runs away from me, sometimes.

I opened Instagram again and looked at the rest of JB's photos. There was one of me and Zack on the beach at the island, grinning at the camera, his arm round my neck. I thought of all the times we'd had our picture taken like that – parties, matches, the one in the common room at school that was currently my profile picture. My mum had a photo of the two of us when we were seven in the same pose. We were dressed in our football kits, me gangly and awkward, Zack with two of his teeth missing. We'd grown up together. In some ways we were like brothers.

But now all I could think about was the way he'd put his arm round me on the boat, his face furious.

The things he had made me do.

THE GUY HAD been difficult to miss from the start – loud and obnoxious on the boat, flashing his dick at a group of girls before we'd even left the shore. His vest top stretched and baggy, chest white and then burnt. Hair slicked back in a quiff. He'd bumped into me and Zack when we first got on, when we were at the bar getting drinks for everyone else. It was crowded on the deck, probably not that big a deal. But when Zack turned round and said, in his typical way, 'Watch yourself, mate,' the guy didn't say, 'Sorry,' or walk off or whatever. He just smirked and said 'How about you watch *your*self? Mate.'

He wouldn't have been the first person to say that to Zack. But I got a bad feeling about him.

Later, in the woods on the island, I hadn't wanted any trouble. It had been a kind of full-on day already and I wasn't feeling myself. When the guy had appeared again and tried it on with Emily and then started with Nate, I just wanted to get away. I didn't care what he called me but it made something burn inside me to see Hope defend me like that. The rest of the day suddenly looked much brighter.

I didn't even pay much attention to his run-in with Zack in the queue to get back on the boat. Everything had that warm edge it gets when you're drunk, and by the time I got there, the guy had disappeared and Zack was shrugging the whole thing off.

But when I saw him on the boat, saw the way this guy's hand lingered as it slipped down Hope's side, the way she smiled up at him like the look on his face meant nothing, I didn't like it. I know I have no right.

I remembered Zack's face close to mine, his arm tightening round my neck as he pulled me down closer. 'You gonna let him get away with that? We've got to teach him a lesson, Logan. We've got to *show* him.' His words pumping through me and everything spinning. All I could think about was that guy's face, his sleazy smile, the word he muttered as he passed me in the woods.

We've got to show *him.*

And when we got off the boat, we saw him drift away from his mates, into an alley beside one of the hotels. I remembered the lights from the dock flashing as we ran, the shadows blurring. The sound of that guy pissing against the bricks.

The way Zack's fist sounded, crashing into his nose.

The blood looked black as it streamed down his face.

I didn't try and stop him. And when the guy got over his shock, when he righted himself and hit Zack back, I didn't do anything then either. When Zack went down, when the guy started kicking him in the ribs, when Zack yelled, 'Logan' –

Yeah, I did something then.

I let my fist hit the guy's face, his stomach, his jaw. I'd winded him and he fell to the ground – I remembered the sound of that too. It had echoed in my ears ever since.

116

It got blurry again then, things spinning. My breath hard in my chest as I leaned against the wall. Zack leaning over the guy, driving his foot into his ribs, over and over. The guy lying there, not moving.

Zack telling me to run. The beach flying past and the blood pounding in my ears.

The guy lying there, not moving.

Lying there in some alley while one of my best friends was passed out by herself on a beach.

Do you hate me yet?

MY PHONE RANG again, and I almost pushed it off the edge of the bed without looking at it. I didn't feel like talking to anyone right then. But the name on the screen caught my eye: Daisy.

Shit, Daisy.

I fumbled the phone as I tried to answer it, rushing it to my ear.

'Hi!'

'I thought you weren't going to pick up,' she said. Her voice was quiet. 'I thought you were still upset with me.'

'No, Dais, I –' I trailed off. I didn't know how to say that the argument we'd had by text when I was away was ridiculous and petty and I didn't care about it, not any more. 'It doesn't matter,' I said. 'I'm sorry, I overreacted.'

'Me too,' she said, sounding relieved. 'Did you have a good time?'

'Yeah.' The last thing I wanted was for Daisy to know about anything that happened in Malia. I didn't want to think about any of it ever again. 'What about you? How's your week been?'

'Pretty boring without you,' she said. I could hear her duvet rustling as she turned over in bed. I knew exactly what she'd been doing, I could picture her so clearly. Curled up in Hogwarts pyjamas, her laptop on the little weird granny tray she had for it – you know, the kind that has like a beanbag underneath it, and is designed for eating dinner in front of the telly. It even had this country-cottage painting on it, and the beanbag bit was covered with a gingham fabric. She got it from a charity shop, I think – half her room was full of weird old antiques and ornaments and jewellery she picked up from charity shops and car boot sales. She'd be watching horror films on Netflix or maybe writing – potentially both.

'How's the next chapter going?' I asked.

'Umm.' I heard her closing the lid of her laptop. 'It's OK. I don't know though.'

'What's up?'

'I guess I just don't want to disappoint people. It was easier when I was the only one who could see it – now I feel like people might not like what happens or they might get bored.'

Just before we'd left for Malia, Daisy had casually mentioned to me that she was writing a novel and that she'd started posting chapters of it online. I was blown away, but then that was always the case with Daisy – we'd been together for six months and still I was finding out all these amazing things she thought and did and never really shouted about.

'Babe, I'm sure they won't. They like what you wrote so far, right?' It was hard for me to be too reassuring, because Daisy still hadn't actually told me much about the novel at all, or even the pseudonym she posted under. I was trying not to let it bother me, trying to understand – if she said she wasn't ready for me to see it yet, that was OK. It had to be.

'I guess so,' Daisy said. 'Anyway. Tell me more about your holiday.'

I had a sudden image of Hope appearing in the doorway. *You left me.* Of some guy whose name I didn't even know lying in an alleyway in the dark.

'Oh,' I said. 'Just a lot of beer and beach really. Actually not that much beach – two of the days we got up too late to get a sun-lounger so we just ended up at our pool.'

'Wild.' I could imagine her rolling onto her stomach as she said it. 'Did Hope have a good time?'

There was no edge to the way she said it. Daisy didn't get jealous. She actually, genuinely wanted to know that Hope had a good time, and that made me feel like someone was twisting a knife in my guts. 'Yeah, I think so,' I said, and I could hear how fake my own voice sounded. 'Probably got a bit bored of being with us lot by the end.'

She laughed. 'Yeah, probably. She's only human. So, you want to do something tomorrow? You could come round, if you want? Everyone'll be out all day.'

Despite everything, the thought of being alone with her made something in me stir. 'That sounds good,' I said. 'I can bring some stuff for lunch, if you like.'

'OK. That sounds nice.' She yawned. 'I'm gonna go. I want to upload this before I go to sleep.'

'OK, babe. Sleep well.'

'You too.'

After we hung up, I turned off my light. I tried to hold on to the thought of Daisy and her laptop on its tray, and to forget all about Greece.

It worked, for a while. I fell asleep.

I SLEPT LATE the next day and only woke up because my phone had buzzed its way across the pillow until it was nudging my head with each notification. I'd dreamt all night of Greek police turning up at the front door, of Mum having to watch as I was dragged out in handcuffs. Of a prison cell, relentlessly hot, where no one could understand me. My eyes felt swollen and it took me a while to focus on my phone screen.

It was Zack, but it wasn't the message I'd been scared of. No police reports surfacing online, no Facebook messages from friends of the guy we'd beaten up who'd somehow tracked us down.

This was just a message to the boys' WhatsApp group. The group's name, chosen by Zack, was, for some reason **Smash The Slut**. It had seemed funny at the time – Zack liked making big over-the-top Keith-Lemon-style sex jokes sometimes, obviously messing around – although it was awkward if anyone else saw the notifications appear on your lock-screen. But that day, then, it made me feel sick. The icon got changed by all of us all of the time – an embarrassing photo of one of the others, or something stupid and cheesy, like Arnie as Rambo or the old *Bad Boys* film poster or whatever. Zack had changed it last, to a picture of some girl in the club in town.

She was dancing with her hands up in the air, eyes closed, and her top had slipped down a bit so that you could see the edge of a nipple.

The conversation was just about some transfer rumour in the Premier League, which had devolved into Zack and Nate hurling insults at each other about how shit their respective teams were. I clicked out of it and lay there, looking at my other messages. One from Daisy:

```
Night xxx.
```

And one from Zack, a private message just between the two of us.

```
Really good holiday pal. Sorry it got
fuked up a bit at the end. x
```

I sighed, looking at it. I knew he didn't always mean to act the way he did. He did care about us all – he'd been around when Hope and me broke up, and when Dev and Mollie did. He just . . . Well, he got out of control sometimes.

Stop blaming him, the little voice in my head said. *He didn't make you do anything. You hit that guy all by yourself.*

I tried to push the thought away. It wasn't exactly like the guy was innocent after all. It wasn't like we'd killed him. Maybe he needed someone to stand up to him.

I opened the group conversation again and scrolled up. JB hadn't written anything since we got back, and Dev was being pretty quiet too. This *thing* between us all, whatever it was, wasn't going away any time soon, no matter how much Zack wanted it to.

I opened a message to Hope and stared for a while at the blinking cursor. I didn't know what to say – *Sorry again that we left you?* Or, *Did something happen that you're not telling me?* Somehow I just couldn't put the bad feeling I had into words – Hope and the guy in the vest and something I couldn't figure out had got all blurred together in my head and I felt guilty without really knowing how to make it OK again. I started typing – *Hey, Hope, how's it going?* – but I sighed and deleted it straight away.

Was it even a good idea for me to be the person checking in with her anyway? Things had already been weird between us after that night outside the club, when she'd leaned in . . .

I pushed that thought away too, because it made my stomach churn. I felt terrible about the way I'd reacted, like it hadn't been exactly what I was thinking too – but I'd panicked. Daisy had popped into my head, as if I'd forgotten all along that she existed, and the shock of it had made me pull back from Hope like she was disgusting.

Except it was me who was disgusting.

I scrolled up through my old messages with her, through the casual, friendly stuff of the last couple of months:

All packed?

                              haha nah course not

I'm sooooo excited!

                    See u at the airport!

and up into the weirder, formal awkwardness of the weeks
after we broke up.

    can u bring my jumper to school tomo

                                    yeh sure

    i don't want this to be weird for either
                                        of us

    me neither but I just need space for a
    bit

I stopped before I got to the couple stuff. No matter what
had happened in Malia, I didn't feel that way about Hope any
more. We worked better as friends, we both knew that. It was
just hard – when you're used to being with someone like that,
it takes a while to reset, to remember you're not supposed to
be kissing or holding hands or thinking that way. I guess being
away had just made us both forget.

    I went back down to the message box and typed, trying not
to think too hard about it.

    hey, hope u slept well. just wanted to
    say again so sorry about the boat night.
    we were shit friends. hope you're ok x

It was lame but it was better than nothing. It made the anxious feeling in my stomach fade a bit at least.

I got up and showered. It felt incredible to be in a clean bathroom again, one that was filled with Mum's flowery, fruity soap and body-wash and shampoo instead of hair and sand and crud from the strip.

We'd moved to the flat three years ago, after Mum and my stepdad, Leon, split up. It wasn't a bad flat, and it wasn't a bad split – they just drifted apart, and we needed somewhere small that Mum could afford on her own. I remembered the day we'd moved in, when Leon drove us here with all our boxes and we sat around in the empty living room eating Chinese takeaway out of tubs. 'You're the man of the house, now, Logan,' Leon had said. 'Got to look after your mum.'

Not that she'd ever needed anyone to look after her – she worked all day behind the desk in a bank and then she spent most of her evenings volunteering at the old people's home on the other side of town, and still managed to have dinner with me most nights and hang out with her friends.

But still, I thought about him saying that a lot. I always felt like I should be doing more. Now it was summer, I needed to get a job, something to add to the kitty. Something that meant I could be the one who brought home a takeaway on Friday nights or who bought Mum her favourite box sets or took her out for Sunday lunch or whatever. Something that meant I was bringing money in and wasn't a kid any more.

OK, so, a job. That felt like a plan, something to focus on, and I felt better, cleaner. There'd been this scummy sort of layer hanging round my head, it felt like – like this weird weight

I couldn't shake off. I put it down to an extended hangover after four nights of hard drinking and promised myself I'd have at least a couple of days of eating every vegetable I could get my hands on.

I got out of the shower and dried myself. Mum had already left for work, so once I was dressed I went to the kitchen to make myself something to eat before I went to meet Daisy. I sat at the narrow little breakfast bar beside the cooker and ate a bowl of cornflakes while looking at my phone again. Still no messages from Dev or JB in the group chat, and no reply from Hope either. She had her profile set so you didn't get the double blue tick when she'd read a message either, so I had no idea if she was still asleep or just ignoring me.

A notification appeared at the top of my screen – a new Facebook friend request from Lucy Terry. I opened it and checked the photo: yep, Malia Lucy. Her picture was her and Rachel by the pool in our hotel, both of them wearing those heart-shaped sunglasses and making peace signs at the camera. I accepted the request because why not, and carried on with my breakfast.

A message came through a couple of minutes later.

```
Hey Logan, thanks for the add! Great to
meet u guys, hope u got back ok? xx
```

I slurped the last of the milk from my bowl and typed a quick reply.

```
Hey! Great to meet you too. Yeah we got
```

```
back all right, all feelin pretty pants
tho :) You guys flew today right? Have a
                         good last night?
```

I clicked back to my home screen and saw a new notification on WhatsApp. Zack had sent some pictures to the group – some of us by the pool, one of all of us on the beach at the island. *What a holiday*, he'd written underneath. No one had replied yet, and I started to feel a bit sorry for him. He was just trying to make things all right again, to remind us how much fun we'd all had before that stupid boat-party night.

I couldn't think about that again. It made me want to smash my head against something hard, over and over.

I took my bowl to the sink and then left. Maybe I'd upload some of my photos later. But for now I was just going to concentrate on Daisy and what she'd like best for lunch. That was something I could get right.

DAISY ANSWERED THE door in leggings and an ancient Hard Rock Cafe T-shirt and the biggest smile I'd ever seen. I leaned in to kiss her and as her hands met behind my head, I wished I could just stay like that forever.

But she pulled away and so instead I held up the paper bags from her favourite fancy deli. 'I bought cheese and the good bread.'

'I love you,' she said, and she pulled me inside and closed the door on the rest of the world.

Later, we were lying on Daisy's bed, watching *Jessica Jones*. Daisy was big on tech and she had a projector screen you could pull down from the ceiling. It covered a whole wall of her room and it was hooked up to her laptop, and she pretty much always had it on, even if she was doing something else – she'd just mute the sound. It was awesome, especially because it pulled down right in between the tall, old-fashioned lamp she'd found at some antiques fair in the town hall and the random hat stand she'd found online. Each of its brass prongs was shaped like an antler, and because Daisy didn't have all that many hats, on the spare ones she'd hung necklaces, scarves, old festival wristbands, a couple of Christmas decorations and a pocket watch her granddad had given her.

'OK, so what kind of thing do you want?' Daisy asked. She'd flopped onto her stomach in front of the laptop, and while *Jessica Jones* was still playing on the wall she had Google open in front of her. 'Do you want something that's, like, CV-useful or just money in the bank?'

'Erm . . . both?'

She turned and rolled her eyes at me before reaching out to dip another bit of bread in the gooey goat's cheese she liked best. 'Yeah, well, the overlap in that Venn diagram is *pretty* small, so, you know, manage your expectations.'

'I don't know, anything I guess,' I said, picking up one of the cushions from behind my head and fiddling with the zip on it. It was an embroidered Marauder's Map and ideal distraction material.

It wasn't exactly like I didn't know what I wanted to do. I knew I wanted to do *something* in an office – something big, like law or business. I wanted to be impressive, I didn't want to ever worry about money. *You're the man of the house now*. But I hadn't thought much past that. I didn't really know what working in business actually meant, despite all the careers leaflets we were handed at school, or how to find out. My uncle had started his own software company in Manchester and made a success of it, but I didn't think I'd be much good at that. I hadn't taken law at AS because I'd heard that universities didn't like that if you were going to do a law degree, but it still felt like a big gamble – what if I was terrible at it and didn't find out until I'd got into uni and started my course?

'So, office temping, maybe?' Daisy said. 'Office experience is always good, my mum says.'

'Yeah, makes sense.'

'Right, well, there's a recruitment agency in town that's looking for temps. They say they've got positions here and in Longhampton. Also in London, but it'd cost you so much to get the train every day it'd be totally pointless, right?'

'Yeah, don't fancy that.'

'OK, well, I'll send you the link to upload your CV – think you have to do a typing test online and stuff.'

'All right, thanks, babe.'

'Let's see what else there is . . . Hmm, that sandwich bar downtown is hiring.'

'Munchies?'

'Yup.'

I pulled a face. 'Not exactly CV stuff, is it?'

She laughed. 'Yeah, course it is! Cash-handling, customer service, blah blah. Plus it's above minimum wage.'

'Hmm, OK . . .' I said, not that convinced. Munchies was a bit of a dive, to be honest. It wasn't the kind of thing I'd had in mind. But it was money and that was the real point of this, right? 'Yeah,' I said. 'Send me the link.'

Daisy clicked decisively a couple of times. 'Done. Oh, there's also a bar job going at the Nelson's Head.'

I thought I'd quite like bar work actually. I'd done a bit of glass collecting last summer at a pub owned by someone Leon knew, and the shifts had always gone by fast. 'Yeah, send me that, too,' I said. I was already looking forward to getting applications sent off. To doing something.

My phone vibrated next to me on the bed, and I glanced at it, assuming it was another set of links from Daisy. But it was a message from Lucy.

```
Haha yeh we did, we ended up goin to
the foam party at Diamond it was sooooo
good! Feels rubbish to b back tho :(
```

A minute later, she followed it up with:

```
hey kno this is a bit forward but u
wanna hang out sometime? I'm at my dad's
in Roehampton this summer, it's easy on
the train. B fun to go for a drink or
something :)
```

'I've got another bar job, this one's at the Wetherspoon's in Longhampton,' Daisy said. 'Interested?'

'Yeah, hit me up,' I said, watching Krysten Ritter slam someone through a wall. I glanced back at Lucy's message again and tapped out a reply.

```
why's that forward lol, sure everyone
would love to see you! Let us know when
you're free and you can come see the
                        sights of Kings Lyme!
```

'How do you feel about retail?' Daisy asked, reaching over to nab another bit of cheese.

'Umm, fine, I guess,' I said. Jessica Jones and Luke Cage were drinking whiskey, barely keeping their hands off each other, and I gave Daisy's foot a squeeze, realising all over again how good it felt to be here with her.

```
oh I kinda just meant me and u ;)
```

What? I glanced at Daisy again. She was distracted by the episode too, watching Jessica and Luke get it on, with her head balanced on her hand.

```
oh right. sorry, I didn't realise. I've
got a girlfriend, and also I wouldn't
                        do that to Dev
```

It took her a couple of minutes to reply, by which time Daisy was busy clicking through job listings again.

```
Dev? what's it got to do with Dev?

            u guys were together in malia!

lol what. we snogged twice on a night
out – one of the times was because I
lost a bet with him!

Huh? He stayed at yours night of the
                            booze cruise

No he didn't! He bottled it and left
after about 5 mins. Boy is clearly still
into his ex. Anyway, you don't have to
use your mate as an excuse, if you don't
fancy me that's totally fine. Just say!
```

I frowned at my phone. That was weird.

```
Like I say, I've got a girlfriend.
Nothing to do with fancying you or not.
                        Have a good week.
```

I felt bad. I probably shouldn't have even replied – what would Daisy think if she saw those messages? But I also didn't want Lucy to feel completely rejected either. She seemed like a nice girl and it was no big deal that she'd asked me out. If anything, I just felt guilty that I clearly hadn't mentioned Daisy to her. Another thing to add to the list of stuff I felt awful about.

'Hey, Dais?' I said, and she looked round at me. 'You don't need to do that. I'll keep looking tomorrow. This is your favourite episode – come and watch it.'

BY FRIDAY, THINGS were starting to feel all right again. Although JB hadn't really said anything on the group since we got back, when Nate sent a message asking if everyone was still up for going round his, he replied to say yes. Seeing his name there felt good, and Dev had been joining in like normal the last couple of days too. In fact, it'd been Dev who'd posted first the day before – a picture of a girl he'd been messaging on Snapchat.

I think I'm in love, the message said. The photo was a picture he'd taken from her profile, of her dressed up for Halloween or something. She was dressed as Harley Quinn, T-shirt ripped and shorts short, pointing her baseball bat at the camera.

Fit, Nate wrote back.

A solid 7, wrote Zack. Then, a minute later, *Maybe a 7.5 if I was drunk*.

I'd usually have joined in. We played this game often enough. Normally I'd just say something about the girl's legs, which looked great in her torn tights, and I started to type. But somehow I just couldn't press send.

But I was glad we were all talking again. And I felt sorry for Dev, especially after what Lucy had said about him bottling it. I didn't know why Dev felt he needed to make up all this stuff about shagging girls when he was clearly still into Mollie. But if it made him feel better, I wasn't going to get in the way of it.

I'd spent the rest of the week applying for jobs, even the Munchies one. There were still four weeks left of summer, so it'd be good to start earning as soon as possible – and, truthfully, I could feel myself getting into a bad routine again, especially with Daisy visiting her grandma up in Scotland for the week. I'd stay up late just clicking through social media or playing Xbox and then end up sleeping all day. It was just normal stuff, but I could feel that weird heaviness coming back. I knew that it wasn't good for me.

I'd had a bad patch last winter. I'd never talked to anyone about it and I still didn't really know exactly what had happened, except that one day, just a random Tuesday, I hadn't wanted to get out of bed. Hope and I hadn't broken up much before that, and I guess I was still sad about it. I missed her, or missed having someone, maybe, and I felt pretty empty. Maybe it's difficult to explain this, but when you feel empty, it really fills up your day. It's hard to find space to make any other thoughts stick, like your brain is just this big bottomless void that you can't find a way out of.

It had just sort of gone away by itself – Mum and me had gone to Manchester to stay with my uncle and aunt and Steph, who could always make me laugh, and while I was there, I'd ended up chatting to Daisy on Facebook one night. We were in a couple of classes together and I'd always thought she was pretty, and once we got talking, we really got on.

Maybe that was just what everyone was like after a break-up – I kept thinking that it wasn't that big a deal, like I was just being a total wimp. But I still remembered how awful it had felt, and I was still always, in a deep, dark corner of my brain, afraid that it might happen again.

So I was glad when it was time to leave for Nate's on Friday night. Daisy was coming back on Sunday evening. And even Hope had replied to me, two days after I'd messaged her.

```
Sorry, just saw this. Don't worry. All
good. Been sleeping alllll week! x
```

It didn't sound exactly like her, but it felt like maybe she'd forgiven us.

When I got to Nate's, Dev and Zack were there, already halfway through a twelve-pack of beer. I added the ones I'd picked up – a bonus of being lanky was that I'd been able to get served since Year 10 – to the fridge and cracked one open for myself.

'Who else is coming?' I asked, sitting down next to Dev.

'JB's on his way,' he said. 'Hope said she might come later too, maybe some of the other girls.'

'Cool.' I looked at him a bit closer. 'You look . . . merry.'

'Yeah. Dhruv took me to the pub this afternoon.' Dhruv was Dev's older brother. He was in his second year at Cardiff University, studying medicine. From the stories Dev told, medical students were pretty wild.

'Where're your parents again, Nate-Dogg?' Zack asked, going to the mantelpiece and picking up a photo of Nate's mum on a beach somewhere.

'Dinner party at an old friend's or something,' Nate said, taking it off him. 'They're staying at some B&B in Surrey.'

'So how's Harley doing, Devdas?' Zack said. 'Nailed her yet?'

Dev finished his beer and reached for another. 'Nah, bro. Playing it cool.'

'Where'd you meet her?' Nate asked. 'And what's her actual name?'

'Lily. She goes to Southfield, I met her at that guy James's party the other week.'

We all raised our eyebrows. Southfield High was the school a couple of towns over, and it didn't have a great reputation, especially over the last couple of years. There'd even been a shooting, when we were in the middle of GCSEs, which meant the area was on the news for weeks. There was still talk about putting metal detectors in at our school.

'Bit of rough, eh?' Zack said. 'Well, whatever floats your boat, mate.'

'How's Daisy, Loges?' Dev asked, clearly keen to change the subject.

'Yeah, she's good.' Her signal was patchy in Scotland so I hadn't heard much from her, but she'd sounded really happy. It was pretty much her favourite place to be in the world. I'd seen pictures – her grandma lived in a cottage on the road to some tiny village with just hills and sky everywhere you looked. The thought made me feel weird and panicked, but for Daisy it was the place she felt calm.

'Shame she couldn't come,' Zack said. 'Feels like it's been ages since we had a full crew together.'

The doorbell rang, right on cue. Nate went to answer it and came back with JB.

'All right, mate,' I said.

'Hi, guys,' JB plonked a six-pack onto the coffee table. 'How's it going?'

'Good, mate,' Zack clapped him on the back. 'Just about recovered. You?'

JB nodded. 'Yeah. My liver's talking to me again at least.'

'Well, tell it to shut up,' Zack said, handing him a beer. 'Right! Who's for a little chaser?' He pulled out a bottle of whiskey.

'Yes, mate!' Dev said, squinting at it. 'Legend!'

'Nice. I'll get some glasses,' Nate said.

I was up for it. But I saw JB sighing. 'It's like six thirty,' he said, sitting down next to me.

I shrugged at him. I really wanted that drink.

Whiskeys poured, Nate held up his glass. 'To summer,' he said.

'To summer.' The whiskey burned the back of my throat but it felt warm in my chest. It felt like relief.

'Right,' Zack said, passing out more beers. 'It's about Ring of Fire o'clock, don't you think?'

'Sounds about right to me,' Nate said, pulling out a pack of cards from under the coffee table and shuffling them. He started splaying them out in a circle, face down on the table, and I cleared some bottles out of the way.

'Don't stitch me up,' Dev said, laughing. He always laughed when he was getting drunk.

I wasn't exactly a big fan of Ring of Fire, which, like Dev said, was mainly designed for stitching each other up. Every card you pulled had some kind of forfeit attached, for you or for someone else in the circle. Everyone who drew a king got to put some kind of drink in the cup in the middle of the circle – except for whoever drew the fourth king, who got to nominate someone to *drink* whatever was in the cup.

I wasn't a big fan. But it did the job. It got you drunk.

'Jesus!' JB shoved his beer away. 'Do we have to?'

'Oooooh.' Zack made a fake surprised face. 'What's up, madam? Can't handle the pace any more?'

JB's face was red. 'Why do we always have to get hammered? Why can't we just do something nice like have dinner or watch a film or something?'

It wasn't just Zack who looked surprised at that. Where was this all coming from?

'Have you ever thought,' JB continued, standing up, 'that maybe it might be nice to actually just have a beer and *talk* to each other every now and again? I can't even remember the last time I had a decent conversation with any of you.'

We all blinked at him. Zack pulled a face, but before he could say anything, the doorbell rang.

'That'll be the girls,' Nate said. 'Chill out, JB, yeah?'

JB sat back down and none of us said anything. He reached out and took his beer and took a big swig.

'He wants a *chat*,' Zack muttered to himself. 'And then we can all do our nails together.'

'Fuck off, Zack,' JB said.

Nate came back with Hope and her friend Charlotte. 'Hey, guys,' Hope said.

'Hopey, how's it going?' Dev wrapped her in a hug. 'Hey, Char.'

'I'll get you some glasses,' Nate said, nodding towards the bottle of wine Hope had in her hand.

'Georgie said she's not gonna make it,' Hope said to JB.

'Something about your mum and David roping her in to help with making props?'

JB rolled his eyes. 'Amateur. I dodged out of that weeks ago. They're in charge of the summer school play again. She'll be up to her elbows in papier mâché until midnight at least.'

'Your parents are so cute.' Hope sat down between us. 'You OK, Logan?'

'Yeah.' I smiled at her. 'How about you?'

Nate came back with two wine glasses and Hope poured drinks for herself and Charlotte. I glanced down at my beer. Empty again. I felt kind of awkward, after JB's outburst and now with Hope there. I found that sips of beer kind of filled the gaps where you should probably be saying words in those situations. It was probably a good job I'd gone for the box of twelve bottles.

'We were just playing Ring of Fire,' Zack said, with a defiant look in JB's direction.

'Yeah, you in?' Dev asked the girls.

Charlotte shrugged. 'Sure.'

Nate picked up the bottle of whiskey and put it on the table. 'May as well make it interesting.'

A couple of hours later, the second round of Ring of Fire had been abandoned. Nate had turned up the music and everyone was just kind of sitting around, having random conversations and laughing at stupid things on phones. I watched Zack and Nate talking about Zack's brother, Freddie, breaking up with his girlfriend and I thought, *See, we do talk to each other*. I went to the fridge to get another beer, and when I came back,

140

Dev was sort of swaying by a bookcase, watching the others. I went over to him.

'You all right, buddy?'

He turned and blinked at me, this really weird expression on his face. 'She's all right, isn't she?'

I glanced in the direction he'd been looking. 'Who, Hope?'

He nodded. The movement made him stumble a bit, and I reached out to steady him before all of Nate's dad's history books hit the floor. 'Yeah, course she is, mate.'

He rubbed uncertainly at his face. I think it was just hitting him how drunk he was. When he looked at me, his eyes were bloodshot. 'I just . . . I feel bad.'

I felt sober then, this cold feeling flowing through me. 'What do you mean?'

'About . . . that night. About what happened.'

'Yeah, well, we all do,' I said, taking another big glug of beer.

He looked at me, chewing his lip, and didn't say anything.

'Dev,' I asked, careful to keep my voice low, 'do you know something I don't? Something that happened that night?'

His eyes went wide and he looked for a second like he was going to cry. He looked *guilty*. 'I just wanted her to have a good time,' he said in a little voice, rocking backwards. I steadied him again.

'Did you do something?'

I still half expected him to say no, I think. We all wanted her to have a good time – nothing Dev was saying was bad. But it was the way he looked as he said it. I just knew.

'Those pills,' he said, his voice even smaller. 'The ones from those Exeter lads.'

I didn't say anything. I just kept looking at him.

141

'They were really good,' he said. 'I just wanted to share. So I put a little bit in her drink.'

'Without her knowing?' I felt sick.

'I thought it'd be funny.' Dev looked like he was going to cry. 'Remember that time Zack did it to all of us at JB's birthday?'

But I was too busy thinking about that night.

'Dev, did you spike me too?'

Dev nodded. By then he was looking at the floor, like some little kid who'd stolen an extra biscuit. 'I guess I got the amount wrong or something,' he said. 'You just puked.' I had a memory of the boat, of leaning over the railing with someone rubbing my back. 'But Hope . . . It fucked Hope up.'

I walked away. I had to walk away. But Dev followed me, stumbling over someone's shoe as he came into the hallway after me.

'Logan, please don't be mad at me. It was for a laugh. I thought it'd be jokes. I didn't know . . .'

'I can't talk to you right now,' I said, pulling on my shoes. My voice was so calm I surprised myself. 'You're drunk. I'm going home and so should you.' He started towards the shoes, one hand to the wall to keep himself upright. 'Not with me,' I said. 'I just need to be on my own right now.'

And I left him standing there.

I'D BEEN LOOKING forward to Daisy getting back all week, but when the day finally came I ended up sleeping through my alarm and had to run most of the way there. By the time I arrived at the shopping centre, sweating and out of breath, I was forty minutes late and Daisy wasn't at the fountain where we usually met.

I fished my phone out of my pocket to call her, but before I hit dial, I heard my name. I spun round and saw her poking her head out of the door to her favourite coffee shop.

I jogged over. 'I'm so sorry.'

Daisy had a seat by the window, her laptop set up. 'Well, thought I'd do some writing.' She typed a couple of words and then lowered the lid of her laptop a bit. 'Did you have a good weekend?'

'Yeah . . .' I didn't really feel like telling her I'd spent most of it trying not to think about what Dev had told me. Trying to ignore the group chat about stupid, pointless things. 'How was Scotland? Do you want another coffee?'

She nodded and then held up the crumb-littered plate next to her. 'Maybe another croissant too?'

I went to the counter, and by the time I got back she was typing again. I put her flat white down next to her and then slid onto the stool opposite.

'Sorry,' she said. 'I wrote two chapters this morning! I'm on a roll.'

'Dais, that's great. Feel like telling me what it's about yet?'

She clicked a few times and then closed the lid decisively. 'Yes, all right.' She picked up her cup and took a sip and then studied me over the top of it. 'But you can't, like, laugh. Or frown. Frowning would really put me off.'

I laughed. 'OK, I won't do either of those things.'

'And don't do that sort of squinty thinking face you do when you don't like something but you're not sure how to say so.'

'My *what* face?'

'You know, like when your mum buys you the wrong socks or the woman in the canteen tries to persuade you to have quiche instead of pizza or whatever. This one.' She wrinkled up her face, head on one side.

'Oh, right. *That* one.' I flicked a croissant crumb at her. 'Fine. No squinty thinking face.'

Daisy took another sip of coffee and then put the cup down. 'OK, so. It's basically like a detective novel, except the stuff she's investigating is all to do with the supernatural. It can be anything – vampire colony in tiny seaside town, demon-summoning ritual in Oxford college, whatever. People come to her when strange stuff's happening, and she goes and figures it out and helps them. *But* she's also like this famous novelist who *writes* novels about all this stuff, so she's kind of hiding in plain sight. She's kind of Sherlock meets Stephen King but with extra Buffy.'

She looked at me. 'You're not making any weird facial expressions.'

'No. I'm not. Because that sounds awesome.'

'Really?'

'Yeah! Can I read it?'

She grinned, slipping her laptop into her bag. 'Yeah, maybe. Come on, let's go.'

As we walked through the shopping centre, I felt light and happy. Daisy took my hand in hers and we walked past all the crappy little carts selling phone covers and sweets and handbags.

'So, what we looking for?' I asked.

'Something for Charlotte for her birthday. And maybe new running shoes if I can find a decent pair for cheapish.'

'OK, cool. I guess I could probably do with some new trainers too.'

She gave me a playful shove. 'You have like twenty pairs!'

'I do not! Anyway, it's my thing.'

She grinned and turned away. 'Let's go look at books for Charlotte.'

In the bookshop, I browsed around the tables while Daisy searched through the fantasy section. I had no idea that Charlotte was even a fantasy fan, even though I'd been friends with her for much longer. But Daisy always knew those kinds of things about people. When it came to her friends, she could probably tell you what their first pet was called and what song they got stuck in their head the most, stuff like that, without even blinking. I thought again about what JB had said that night at Nate's. *I can't remember the last time I had a decent conversation with any of you*. I pulled out my phone to send him a message – just to say hey or whatever.

'I'm going to get her this,' Daisy said, interrupting my thoughts. I put my phone away and looked at the book. I didn't recognise the title or the author – I didn't read any fantasy, and right then I wasn't reading anything much at all. I found it hard to keep my attention on the words on the page, and usually I ended up falling asleep or playing on my phone. But I didn't want Daisy to know that, and the cover was nice, so I nodded like I knew what I was talking about. 'Cool.'

'She loves this series,' Daisy said, 'and this one's just out. Come on, help me pick a card.'

We left the bookshop and carried on drifting through the mall. 'Did you hear anything about those jobs?' Daisy asked.

I shook my head. 'Not yet.'

'Oh,' she said, frowning. 'That's weird. Well, never mind. I'm sure they'll get back to you soon.'

'Yeah, probably.' Thinking about it gave me an uncomfortable feeling in my chest and I realised I didn't really want to talk about it right then. 'So, results day next week. Want to go in together?'

'Yep, that'd be nice.' She glanced at me. 'You nervous?'

'Nah.' I realised right away that I probably was. 'It's just AS's, right? No big deal. Anyway, I feel like the exams went pretty well.'

Daisy nodded. 'Yeah, you'll be fine. You're annoyingly clever, given you never bother studying.'

'Can't help it,' I said, tapping my temple with a finger. 'Photographic memory.'

She shoved me, rolling her eyes, and then I pulled her back towards me and we walked for a while like that, my arm around her shoulder.

'Shall we get one?' Daisy said as we passed the little hut selling frozen yoghurt. 'I'm buying.'

'I'll get them,' I said, even though they were stupidly overpriced. 'What flavour do you want?'

Dev had once told me off for letting Daisy buy stuff all the time. 'You're supposed to treat them like a princess,' he'd said. 'Don't make the same mistake I did with Mollie.' I didn't think Daisy cared about stuff like that, but I did want to make her feel special. Looked after. That was what men were supposed to do, right?

Daisy went to sit on the edge of the fountain, so I ordered the cones – mango (urgh) and toffee chips for Daisy, strawberry and white chocolate sauce for me – and took them over to her. As I sat down, my phone buzzed with a new message. Dev.

```
feel sick bout what i sed the other
night. dunno what to do.
```

I put my phone back in my pocket without replying. You and me both, I felt like saying. I'd managed to distract myself all day with Daisy, but now I couldn't get the image of Dev crumbling a pill into Hope's drink out of my head. Suddenly I didn't want to eat the cone I'd just bought.

'You OK?' Daisy asked, wiping a drip of strawberry off the back of my hand where I hadn't even noticed it melting.

I knew I should tell her. Daisy would know the exact right thing to do; she'd know whether I should tell Hope or make Dev tell Hope or just leave the whole thing well alone.

But when I looked at her, I couldn't do it. I didn't want her to think of all of us out in Malia behaving like that. How could I sit there with her and talk about what an awful person Dev was, when her boyfriend was the kind of guy who attacked someone, two against one, in some dark alleyway?

'Yeah,' I said, 'I'm fine. Just kind of full. You want some of this?'

THE NEXT DAY, I woke up to an email from the temp agency, thanking me for my application but saying that they were no longer looking for new candidates for their books. Nothing from the pubs or the sandwich place.

In the kitchen there was a note from Mum saying she'd taken on an extra shift at the care home that evening, with a folded twenty for a pizza.

I decided to go back to bed for a while.

BED WAS MY friend for the next few days too. I was tired, more tired than I'd realised, and I put that down to a lingering hangover from Malia. What was the harm in chilling out for a bit? Getting some extra sleep and catching up on Netflix stuff seemed like the best thing to do. It wasn't like I had anything else to do.

On Wednesday night there was an England friendly on telly, so we'd all arranged to watch it at the Wheatsheaf, this big soulless pub next to the supermarket on the outskirts of town. It was hardly ever busy, which meant they hadn't been ID-ing us for a couple of years. When I arrived, Nate and Dev had baggsied a big table with a good view of the screen.

I waved at the two of them and went to the bar to buy myself a pint, delaying the moment I'd have to go over. I hadn't really spoken to Dev since Nate's. After staring at his message for ages the night before, I'd ended up replying:

    it was a messed up thing to do, but it's
                                done now.

It was a complete cop-out, and I knew it. I just got this feeling that Hope didn't want to talk or think about that night, and

I didn't know if I could handle any more rifts in the group. I couldn't bring myself to force Dev to tell the truth or apologise.

But at the same time I couldn't help thinking about how he'd lied to us about where he'd stayed that night. I couldn't help thinking how weird it was that JB and Nate had also supposedly disappeared off with random people. I didn't know why, but something just felt totally off about the whole thing.

I didn't know what I was thinking, getting suspicious of my best mates. My brain felt like it was trying to hear and see things through a thick grey fog. Then again, it wasn't exactly like I didn't have my own secrets to hide.

'All right, mate?' JB appeared next to me just as I was getting served. 'Here, I'll get that.'

'Cheers.' I smiled at him. 'How's it going?'

'Yeah, all right.' He held up his hands, which were spattered with paint. 'Guess who got roped into last-minute play preparations with Mum and David?'

I laughed. 'Unlucky.'

'Here you go.' He handed me my pint. 'Well . . .' He glanced in the direction of the table. I got the feeling I wasn't the only one feeling less than social.

'Come on.' I made my way over to the others, JB behind me. Zack had arrived while we were at the bar, and he stood up and gave us both his half-handshake, half-low-five thing.

'Sorry, Z, didn't realise you were here,' JB said. 'Let me get you a drink.'

'Nah, no worries, mate. I'll go. Anyone else need anything?'

No one did. I sat on the stool next to Nate, avoiding Dev's eye. JB took the one opposite and started telling us all about the cardboard palm trees he'd been making for his mum's play. 'David wants to hang actual coconuts from them but they just keep drooping,' he said, laughing. 'No one likes a droopy set of coconuts, do they?'

The whistle for kick-off blew just as Zack came back with his beer. 'I fancy our chances here, boys,' he said. 'Could easily do them 3–0, I reckon.'

'Don't underestimate that defence,' JB said. 'It'll be harder than you think, from their last couple of games.'

We watched the screen, sipping our drinks and making the occasional comment – or criticism. It felt like a familiar rhythm and I began to relax. One drink down, I felt fuzzier but like the fog was lifting.

'Another, Loge-Dogg?' Zack got up from the table.

'Yeah, cheers – I'll get the next ones.'

He waved that away – it wasn't like he was short of money. Zack's dad had given him a credit card as soon as he turned sixteen, the same as he'd done for Freddie two years before. No questions asked, bills barely glanced at. Zack could afford to be generous – but he always was, without even thinking about it. To him, things weren't fun unless he could share them, it never occurred to him to keep stuff for himself.

While he was at the bar, England conceded a penalty, sending the whole room into a round of irritable muttering. It was only a friendly, but people were already gearing up to say how terrible the new manager was.

'Told you,' JB said. 'They're a tight team – we've gone in way too complacent.'

'We're playing like a bunch of women,' Zack said, putting

152

down the pints he'd balanced carefully between his hands. He jogged back to the bar to collect the last one and then sank back into his seat, eyes on the screen. 'Bloody hell, Hastings, grow some balls!'

We all watched in silence as our striker bottled another tackle.

'Don't fancy our chances in the Euros then,' Nate muttered, pulling one of the fresh pints towards him. 'Cheers, Zack.'

Dev reached out to take his drink too, and I couldn't help glancing at him. He caught my eye and smiled awkwardly, and I thought of him swaying in the corner of Nate's living room, watching Hope. *I just wanted her to have a good time.* I looked away.

At half-time it was still 1–0 and the players were looking a bit bewildered at how totally unimpressive they were. We turned away from the screen and huddled into our drinks.

'It was a good night on Friday,' Zack said. 'Not that you'd know, Logan, abandoning us like that.' He grinned at me to show he was joking, and I didn't smile back.

'Yeah, it was fun,' Nate said. 'And nice to see the girls too.'

'Yeah, glad Novak's over her hissy fit,' Zack said, draining his drink. 'She was on good form, Friday.'

I saw JB's hand tighten round his glass and I looked down at the table. *Don't say anything*, I thought. *Don't waste your time.*

But JB clearly wasn't receiving psychic messages at that point.

'It's hardly a hissy fit to be upset when your friends leave you passed out on a foreign beach,' he said. 'I think it's pretty normal to be upset about that. I think it's pretty horrific behaviour, to be honest.'

'Oh, have a day *off*, JB!' Zack said. 'I'm so sick of hearing about this. Seriously, what is your deal?'

'My "deal" is that we acted like a pack of animals out there and one of our friends could've been seriously hurt because of it. You have no idea what happened; she has no ide—' JB, whose face had gone all red, cut himself off, clearly thinking better of it. 'Look, the point is, we're friends. We're supposed to look out for each other. You know, like, take *care* of each other?'

'What are you, gay?' Zack said, laughing, but JB put his pint down. He wasn't laughing.

'Yeah, I am actually.'

Zack was still laughing. 'Yeah, OK.' There was a long silence. Zack looked up and saw JB's face. 'What, you serious?'

'Yes, Zack. I'm serious.'

'But . . . You can't be. You –' Zack looked from JB's pint to the screen to all of us.

'Yes, Zack,' JB said again. His voice was perfectly calm. 'I like football and beer and I fancy boys. I know that's going to be a difficult concept for you to get your head round.'

Zack just stared at him.

'Well, I think that's cool,' Nate said awkwardly, breaking the silence. He offered JB a handshake. 'Are we meant to say congrats? How does coming out even work?'

JB laughed. 'I dunno. But thanks.'

I just went for a hug. I didn't know what to say really, especially with Zack sitting across the table with his jaw flapping. It wasn't a big deal to me – but I didn't want to *say*, 'Hey, no big deal,' because it was clearly a huge moment for JB. So instead I panicked and said nothing. Words were failing me again, just like they always do. I wished Daisy was there.

'I'll erm . . . I'll get us some more drinks,' Dev said, getting up from the table. Zack followed him to the bar without a word.

We watched the second half without talking much. And when it was over, we left without saying much either.

I WAS GETTING bad again. I could feel it coming in like storm clouds crossing a sea, but I didn't want to admit it to myself. I didn't want it to be true. But every day getting out of bed felt like some kind of Olympic effort, and the idea of opening the curtains felt like running a marathon. I slept each day until gone lunchtime, but then at night I'd lie awake until the sky started to lighten, clicking endlessly through web pages without really reading them.

I read all the messages on the boys' WhatsApp group but I never replied. Thinking of funny things to say took too much energy.

I made excuses to Daisy too – I told her I was seeing the boys, or having dinner with Mum. I didn't know why. I just felt like I needed to be on my own.

I knew it was bad when I couldn't sleep one night and ended up with a bottle of Bacardi out of Mum's drinks cabinet. Just lying there on my bed, drinking Bacardi out of a mug. Lying there with the same old thoughts circling through my head. All week I'd been wanting to google news in Malia, wanting to know that the guy me and Zack beat up was OK. Up until then I'd been scared. But with two mugs of Bacardi down me, I found myself wanting to find out once and for all. I couldn't shake the feeling that if I at least knew he was OK, everything else might start to slot back into the way it used to be.

So I opened my laptop and tried searching 'Attack Malia July 2017'. I took a big swig of Bacardi before I looked at the results.

But there was nothing there – well, there were plenty of results about a bar called Attack on the strip somewhere. And a couple of random blog posts about people getting in fights and something called 'Attack of the slags!' which I didn't bother clicking on.

I tried 'Police Malia' and filtered for stuff posted in the past month. As I scrolled down the first few, I started to feel calmer. There were a couple of articles about a police crackdown on drinking in the street, and then a video of a group of lads dancing to Bruno Mars with two police officers outside a club.

But then I hit the bottom of the first page of results, and my stomach dropped.

Police appeal for information after UK tourist reported missing in Malia

Crete police have been interviewing holidaymakers in popular party spot after a UK national was reported missing

That was all I could see in the preview, and it took me a couple of deep breaths and another big glug of Bacardi before I could get the courage to click on the article itself. What if the guy had died? What if he'd never made it out of that alley – what if he was still *there*?

My heart started beating double-time when I saw the date

of the article. It was the day we'd flown back, two days after the boat party. About the right time for the news to break over here, maybe? The words danced in front of my eyes and it took me a while to calm down enough to read them.

Crete police have been interviewing holidaymakers in Malia, a popular holiday destination on the island of Crete, after a UK tourist was reported missing there on Sunday. The British Embassy in Athens said they were aware of the investigation and that they were 'doing everything they can to support it'.

The tourist, whose name has not been released until her family can be reached, was said to have been on holiday with a group of friends. Another British holidaymaker, who asked not to be named, said that the woman had attended a party on a yacht, organised by local company Party Boat, on the day of her disappearance. Police in Crete refused to confirm or deny this at this time.

I read it again, trying to feel relieved. It wasn't anything to do with me and Zack after all. But it was pretty disturbing that some girl had gone missing after the boat party. I couldn't get the image of Hope asleep on the beach out of my head. What if something had happened to her instead?

I closed my laptop and hit the light switch too. I wanted to sleep. I didn't want to think about any of this.

But it took a long time for sleep to come. Hearing that a

girl had gone missing that night just made me feel even worse about us leaving Hope behind, and that kept spiralling into other things I could feel bad about – everything from the fact I didn't have any money to me not reading Daisy's novel yet. I just lay there, mentally kicking myself for hours.

I knew I needed to force myself out of the house. So the next day, when Zack messaged to ask all of us if we wanted to play five-a-side, I said yes.

When I turned up at the outdoor centre I was feeling pretty good. It was a warm day and it was nice to be outside, now that I'd made it past my front door. By the time I hit the road leading to the centre, I felt like the fog was lifting – just a little bit. And I knew it'd be good to be with the boys. I felt like I hadn't said a word out loud for days. They were sitting in my chest, this big heavy tangle of them.

But when I rounded the corner to the pitch, Zack was there with his rugby mate, Marcus, and Nate and Dev were standing there looking awkward.

'Where's JB?' I asked.

Zack shrugged. 'Marcus wanted to play.'

Nate chucked a ball at me. 'Come on, let's just get in there.'

So we played a match against a team from Abbots Grey, but the mood was subdued and I fumbled the ball a couple of times. One of their players was some kid who'd been scouted by Norwich and he ran rings round the rest of us – by the time the whistle went for full-time, we'd lost 7–1.

'What's with you?' Zack asked me as we were getting our stuff. 'You're not on your game at all.'

I shrugged. 'Just think it's out of order you didn't invite JB.'

'Oh, boo-hoo,' Zack said. 'It's no big deal, get over it.'

'You guys want to go get a burger or something?' I noticed Dev looking at me hopefully, even though he was asking all of us.

'Yeah, all right,' Nate said.

'We're in,' Zack said, clapping Marcus on the back. 'Gotta keep the protein levels up.'

But I shook my head. 'I've gotta get back. Promised Mum I'd help her with something.'

I walked home slowly, my kit bag heavy in my hand. The word-lump was still in my chest – if anything it was knotted tighter.

ONE AFTERNOON I was playing Xbox, a half-eaten extra-large pizza in its box on the bed beside me. I'd only been awake for an hour or so, and the pizza was from the night before. All in all, it wasn't a particularly eventful day.

I was just considering whether I wanted to go for a fourth slice when my phone vibrated on the bedside table.

It was a new message on WhatsApp. *Zack Conway added you to the group* **Laaaaaaads**. I clicked on it.

```
All right boys. thinkin' we should start
planning Ibiza for next summer? Will be
bants
```

Jeez, we'd only been back for a fortnight. And Ibiza sounded pricey. I refreshed my email on the off-chance someone had decided to offer me a job in the last three hours. No such luck.

I opened the group again. Someone had replied.

```
Yes braaaaah. Sounds awesome
```

It had come up with a number I didn't recognise instead of a name. I frowned. Had one of the others changed their number?

I tapped on the group info and scrolled down to the member details. Zack, me, Dev, Nate and the random number. That random number's icon was a scrum, and its status was *That's King Marcus to you, peasant.*

Marcus. Zack had added Marcus and not JB.

I shook my head, scrolling through to see if I could add him. But Zack was the only admin for the group.

I tapped the phone against my head, thinking. I should just call Zack up and ask him outright what he thought he was doing.

Before I could, my phone starting vibrating in my hand. I glanced at the screen.

Steph wants to FaceTime with you.

I stared at it for a second. I loved my cousin, but I wasn't sure I was ready for her enthusiasm. On the other hand – I glanced around my room, at the piles of clothes on the floor, the closed curtains – maybe that was exactly what I needed.

I sat up properly and swiped to answer the call.

My phone blinked and then switched to Steph's face, pressed as close to the phone as she could get it, so that a large proportion of the screen was the view up her nose. I burst out laughing.

'Lovely.'

'Hey, cuz,' she said, pulling back and propping the phone up so I could see her properly. 'How's it going?'

'Yeah, all right. How are you?'

'Well, you know. Fighting off adulthood with every available limb. So how was Malia? So glad you didn't drown in a fishbowl or whatever.'

162

'Yeah, it was good.' I changed the subject as quickly as possible. 'How's work?'

Steph had just started working at a shoe shop in the Arndale Centre. She was hoping to be a teacher eventually, but she couldn't decide whether to save up for uni now or try to get a job as a teaching assistant. She was only a year older than me but somehow that gap was starting to feel bigger and bigger. She was making decisions about her actual life – talking about one day moving into her own place with her boyfriend, Deano, and where they wanted to live and where she might go to study. The only decisions I seemed to be making were which toppings to have on my pizza; whether to go for wedges or curly fries.

'Oh my God, Logan, I swear – if I have to measure one more screaming toddler's foot I will actually pull my ovaries right out on the shop floor and stamp on them.'

'Again, lovely.'

'Sorry.' Steph looked away from the phone and started fluffing her hair up in the mirror. 'How's Daisy?'

'Yeah, she's good. She's writing a novel.'

'Oh my God, amazing! I love her.'

I rolled my eyes. 'You love everyone.'

'Not true. I'm very selective. I'm not that keen on you, if I'm honest.'

I laughed. 'Charming.'

Steph picked up her phone. 'Oh my God, you have to see Dad's new toy.' She was walking through their house, which I knew as well as my own flat – better, in fact, since I'd been going to theirs since I was three years old. I got a glimpse of a painting my Auntie Yvonne had done when we were kids. It was of a row of beach huts in Brighton, where me and Mum and Leon had gone on holiday with Uncle Darius, Auntie Yvonne and Steph. I remembered running across the pebble beach and huddling into a carriage on the waltzers on the pier. It was a good holiday – we had a framed photo of all six of us on the windowsill in the lounge.

Steph passed through the kitchen, which was painted lime green and peach, packed full of cookbooks and paella pans and tagine dishes and woks – Uncle Darius loved cooking.

'Say hi to Mum!' she said, flicking the phone in the direction of the fridge, where Auntie Yvonne was taking the milk out of the door.

'Hiya!' I yelled.

'Hi, darling! Did you have a good holiday?'

Steph had already whipped the phone back round to her own face, but I called, 'Yes, thank you,' anyway. Steph danced me through the lounge, flipping the phone round to show me Dougal, the ancient family dog, flopped out on the sofa.

'Hey, Doogs,' I said.

And then Steph was out of the back door and into their narrow garden. 'Look!'

I squinted at the screen. 'What . . . is that?'

'That, my friend, is a potter's wheel.'

'A what now?'

The image blurred into a swirl of bricks, and then my uncle Darius's face appeared. 'You make pottery on it, Logan. I thought you were meant to be the smart one of the family.'

'Hey, Uncle D. You taking up pottery now, then?'

'Yep. Can I interest you in a vase of some kind? Decorative plate?'

'Dad, you're getting clay alllll over my phone,' Steph said in the background.

'I'm good, thanks, Uncle D,' I said, trying not to laugh. 'I'm sure Mum would appreciate something for Christmas though.'

Darius had a habit of picking up new hobbies. He was kind of an overachiever, and not particularly good at 'downtime'. He drove Auntie Yvonne mad.

'Everything good with you?' he asked me. 'You taking care of your mother?'

'Trying to.'

Uncle Darius's face crinkled in a smile. 'Good man.'

'Anyway, got to go,' Steph said, grabbing the phone back. 'Big love, Logey.'

'Bye,' I said, and she blew me a kiss and then hung up.

I looked at my phone for a second and then I opened the browser. The article about the girl going missing had been playing on my mind a lot, and I knew I needed to find out more about her. I typed 'girl missing malia' and limited the dates again.

This time the first entry was exactly what I was looking for.

Student, 18, missing after holiday in Malia
Friends raised the alarm when Emily Simpson, from Sussex, didn't return to her hotel room after a night out.

I clicked on it without paying much attention to the name – but when the article loaded, I almost dropped my phone. There

165

was a photo alongside it, and it was *Emily*, the Emily Hope had made friends with on the island. The one we'd all spent half the day with.

And now she was missing.

I read the rest of the article, my mouth dry.

The friends and family of Emily Simpson are appealing for anyone to come forward if they saw her on the night of 17th July. Emily was last seen leaving the beach at just after midnight, having been on an organised boat party that afternoon. She told friends that she was planning to visit a bar they had previously been to, and would meet them back at their apartment later that evening.

Her friends alerted local police the following lunchtime, after Emily failed to return.

A police spokesperson said that they were currently exploring the possibility that Emily had left voluntarily or whether another party had been involved.

Emily's parents were not available for comment, but a friend of the family said, 'Emily is a responsible, caring girl, who wouldn't disappear without letting anyone know where she was going. This is very worrying indeed.'

I copied and pasted the link and sent it to the group, and then opened a message to Hope. I hadn't seen her since the night at Nate's – and I'd ended up hardly talking to her even then. But I knew she'd want to know about this.

Or would she? It wasn't exactly like she wanted to be reminded of that night, especially now it turned out something had happened to a girl she'd been hanging out with.

A new message slid down from the top of my screen – JB replying on the group.

```
omg that's awful
does Hope know?
```

```
                    I was just messaging her
```

I stared at the screen for a second. I sort of wanted to ask JB what I should say, but that felt pathetic. Hope used to be my girlfriend after all. But before I had time to write anything else, JB messaged again.

```
maybe I should call her
Think she'll be quite upset
```

```
                                    yeah ok
```

I felt a bit useless. But I knew he was right.

```
                            good plan
```

None of the others wrote anything at all.

THE NIGHT BEFORE results day, I stayed up until 4 a.m., working my way through a six-pack of beer and reading sports news online. I couldn't stop thinking about Emily and I didn't know why. I'd only met her for a couple of hours; why was it bothering me so much? I couldn't tell if thinking about her disappearing was causing my sleepless night, or if me not being able to sleep was just giving me plenty of space to think endlessly about things. Either way, all night the sinking feeling in my stomach from the day before wouldn't go away.

I kept running over that night, thinking about what happened after we all got off the boat. Zack and I had run after the guy in the vest top, and after that we'd walked back up the beach to the hotel. I'd gone to bed, head spinning, and fallen asleep, and when I woke up, the others were already up and about in the living room.

JB claimed he'd gone to the strip with people he'd met on the beach, and I'd seen Nate stagger off in that direction too. But it had always seemed weird to me that he couldn't remember anything at all – Nate hardly ever suffered from blackouts; he was usually the person who filled in the blanks for everyone else the next day.

Then again, maybe Dev had spiked his drink too. Dev, who

claimed to have spent the night with Lucy but hadn't. What else was he lying about?

I knew I was being crazy. But, like I say, I had a lot of time on my hands. And I'd never been able to shake the feeling that the others were trying to keep me in the dark about that night.

So I drank my beer. I read my articles. I tried not to think.

When I woke up, I had a headache and the heavy feeling was worse.

I lived on one side of the college and Daisy lived in the opposite direction, so we'd arranged to meet outside the gates. She was already there when I arrived, wearing vintage Aviators and her favourite jeans. When she saw me coming, she slid her phone back into her satchel.

'Hey,' she said, stretching up to give me a kiss. 'How you doing, stranger?'

I smiled. 'I'm OK. I missed you.'

'You've been pretty busy lately.'

I felt sick. I was lying to my girlfriend – and what kind of guy didn't want to see his girlfriend anyway? In some ways, I wanted to talk to her so badly. My head felt like a swamp where I was slowly drowning, and I knew Daisy might actually be the one person who could help me make sense of it – but the idea of putting together the words to try to explain how I was feeling, the things I was thinking, seemed insane.

'I'm sorry,' I said. 'I'll make it up to you.'

She shrugged. 'Hey, guess what? I hit twenty thousand reads!'

'Whoa, Daisy, that's huge!'

She grinned. 'The website put me on the 'Featured' page last week and it just went crazy. I'm so happy.'

'I'm really proud of you.'

'Thanks.' She held out her hand. 'C'mon, let's go do this.'

We walked through the front doors and headed for the common room, which had been set up for results day. They'd cleared out all the ratty sofas and the table football and then set up desks at either end of the space – one for AS results and one for A2s. I saw Dev standing to one side with Charlotte, and they both spotted us and waved. We made our way over.

Dev was already clutching his envelope. 'Two Cs, a D and a B,' he said. 'Guess I'm not off to join Dhruv at med school, right?'

He was kidding. Dev had no interest in studying medicine. He was only sticking with A levels to get his parents off his back, same as Nate.

'That's pretty good, mate,' I said. 'What was your D in?' It surprised me, hearing my voice. It sounded so normal, but I felt like it was taking me twice the usual effort to heave each word out. At least here, in daylight and in the all too familiar surroundings of school, I realised how completely ridiculous it was to suspect my friends of having anything to do with Emily Simpson going missing.

'Biology,' he said. 'I'm dropping it anyway. Turns out I know less about the body than I thought, eh, ladies?' He waggled his eyebrows and Charlotte groaned and turned away.

'How'd you do, hun?' Daisy asked her.

'Two As, two Bs,' Charlotte said, and Daisy squealed and hugged her.

'That's brilliant!'

'Well in, Char,' Nate said, coming up behind us.

'Thanks.' She smiled, looking down at her envelope. 'I'd better get going. My mum's waiting outside in the car.'

'See ya, Char,' I said, and then Daisy tugged on my arm.

'Guess we may as well get it over with,' Nate said, patting me on the back. 'I already know I'm resitting history.'

I nodded. I could tell from the way Nate was looking at me that he could see something was up, but he just gave me another pat and then turned away. We headed over to join the queue, where Zack was already at the front, his phone in his hand. He turned as they handed him the envelope and noticed us.

'Hey!' He came over. 'Loges, you all right?'

He seemed genuinely happy to see me, which just made the churning guilt in my stomach that extra bit worse. 'Yeah, I'm good, man. How'd you get on?'

Zack shrugged. 'Haven't checked yet, hang on.' He tore the top off his envelope and pulled out the sheet of paper inside. 'Four Bs,' he said, sounding surprised. He looked up at me, a grin spreading across his face. 'Four Bs!'

I couldn't help smiling back at him. 'That's great, mate. Well done.'

'I've gotta go call my dad!' he said. 'Can't bloody believe it!'

He disappeared off down the steps and I glanced at Daisy, who grinned at me.

'Bless him,' she said. 'That'll be you in a second.'

'Ha. Maybe.' If I was honest, I was hoping for a couple of As. I'd always done pretty well at school – not, like, top of every class, but always up there, always getting decent marks. I'd found exams a bit harder than I was expecting, but I felt like I knew enough to get me through.

The queue moved forward again so that there were only a couple of people ahead of us. Someone tapped my shoulder, and I turned round and saw JB.

'All right, dude,' he said. 'How's it going?'

'Good, yeah. How are you? Nervous?'

JB shrugged. 'Kinda. Pretty sure I flunked chem.'

'Nah. Come on, you studied so hard.'

'Yeah. Well, too late to worry now, eh? Hey, Dais.'

'Hi.' She gave him a hug. 'Really happy for you, by the way.'

'Thanks.' He gave me an uncertain look. 'Guess I kind of dropped a bombshell on everyone, huh?'

I shook my head. 'Not at all, mate. I think it's great.'

JB smiled. 'It feels good now I've said it. It was, like, you guys are my oldest friends – why aren't I telling you something so important about myself? Why am I even scared?'

'Yeah.' I gave him a hug. 'I'm glad you did. You shouldn't have been scared.'

'Next?'

The people in front had collected their envelopes and my business-studies teacher, Mr Langdon, was looking at us. 'Oh, Logan. Hold on –' He rifled through a pile of envelopes in front of him. 'Here we are.'

'Thanks, Mr L.'

'Good luck.'

I stepped away from the table and waited while Daisy and JB collected theirs. Dev came over and nudged me.

'Logan, we're cool, right?' he said.

I glanced at him and then back at Daisy, who was already tearing open her envelope as she came towards us. I felt stupid for holding on to mine, making a big deal out of it.

'How'd you do, babe?' I asked.

Her eyes flicked across the page. 'Three As and a B!'

'Nice one!' Dev high-fived her and then she flung her arms round me. I hugged her tight, not wanting to let go.

JB was reading his results. 'An A, two Bs and a C,' he said, with obvious relief. 'Good job I'm dropping chem though.'

'Well done, mate,' I said, clapping him on the back, and then I realised they were all looking at me. Not my favourite thing at the best of times.

'Come on then, open it,' JB said, grinning at me. 'You'll be fine.'

'You can wait if you want,' Daisy said. 'You don't have to do it with all of us watching.'

'No, it's fine.' I knew I should just get it over with. It's not like I was worried or anything. I slid my finger under the flap of the envelope and dragged it open. The piece of paper felt thin and cheap in my hand. I unfolded it and read – I was so conscious of their eyes on me that it took me a second to line up the characters on the page and translate them into words.

'Logan?'

I looked up at Daisy and realised I'd been quiet for longer than was comfortable. 'Two Bs and two Cs,' I said.

'Hey, that's great,' JB said. 'Well done, man.'

'Yeah, good work, Logester,' Dev said.

'Thanks.' I shoved the paper back into the envelope. 'Shall we go?'

As we walked back out towards the car park, I started to feel numb. I knew those results were fine, good in fact, especially given I hadn't tried particularly hard. But I hadn't been expecting them – I know that sounds stupid now. I know that makes me sound like an idiot. But, I don't know, I'd just always got by on being reasonably clever – and now, suddenly, that hadn't been enough. I'd been expecting to have some big celebration and a couple of As under my belt but instead I'd got my first ever Cs. And I had no one to blame but myself.

'Hey! Logan!'

I glanced up. Zack was standing by his dad's car, about to get in the passenger side. 'How'd you do, mate?'

I did a weird kind of thumbs-up thing.

'Want to come over tonight and have a few beers?'

I hesitated. 'Um . . . yeah. OK.'

'Cool. You too, Dev-Dogg!'

And then he climbed into the car and Gordon sped off in his usual show-off style. Zack hadn't even looked in JB's direction.

'What the fuck was that?' Daisy asked. I glanced at JB, who just shrugged.

'It's fine,' he said. 'Don't worry about it, mate.'

I TRIED TO persuade JB to come to Zack's that night anyway, but he said he wanted to hang out with Georgie and their parents. They were going for a pizza at the new Italian place in town, or so he said, and Josh was going with them. It was kind of a big deal because he hadn't met the rest of the family yet, apart from JB, who wasn't his biggest fan. I hadn't really seen Georgie since the two of them got together – I knew it had caused a bit of tension with Charlotte, and that that was how the girls' holiday had ended up getting cancelled. How Hope had ended up on ours. Other than that, I hadn't taken much interest.

Daisy's parents were taking her out for dinner too, and she'd asked me if I wanted to go – but I knew she was just being nice. It wasn't that her parents didn't like me; they seemed to, and they were always really polite to me. But I still didn't feel like I knew them all that well, and this was a special occasion for them – they were really proud of pretty much everything Daisy did. I didn't want to get in the way.

And, OK, if I'm being honest, I wanted to get drunk.

Mum was working when I got home from collecting my results, but when I got out of the shower that evening I heard her calling for me as she came in the front door.

175

'You're home early,' I said, coming to the bathroom door in my towel.

'Wanted to hear about your results,' she said, smiling at me. 'I would've called on my lunch but this piece of junk had no battery again. You're going to have to help me pick a new one.' She tossed her phone onto the hall table. 'So come on then. How'd you get on?'

I swallowed. It wasn't like Mum was the kind of parent who pushed for perfect grades or would cry if I didn't go to Cambridge. She expected me to do my best and that was it. No matter what I said at that moment, she'd probably tell me, 'Well done,' and then make me a cup of tea or even offer me a beer.

But somehow I heard myself saying, 'Two As and two Bs.'

Because I wanted to see that smile spread across her face. I wanted to hear her say, 'Wow, that's great!'

Because I'm weak.

I left the house an hour later, after Mum had broken out a dusty bottle of prosecco from the cupboard. It tasted like ash in my mouth and I'd had to keep a smile on my face – while inside, the whole time, I was kicking myself. Why had I said that? Why had I lied? Two Bs and two Cs were perfectly good results – why hadn't I just told her the truth?

But I knew why. It was because I'd let myself down by not studying. I was ashamed. And so I drank a glass of prosecco and then another and then I made my excuses and left – but not before Mum had promised we'd go out to dinner at the weekend to celebrate.

'This is exactly what the Rainy Day Fund is for,' she'd said,

176

a bit fuzzy-eyed from her third glass of prosecco. 'We'll go to that new pizza place or something, push the boat out.'

And of course that made me feel really great. As I walked to Zack's, I felt like the lowest person alive. I knew I'd have to tell Mum the truth, and I knew she wouldn't understand why I'd lied.

Before that had to happen, there was beer.

Zack's family lived in a massive house right near the centre of town. There were steps up to it from the street, and a huge double front door. I rang the bell and listened to it echo inside the house. Zack's mum answered, her hair in a towel and a glass of champagne in her hand. 'Hello, love. Go on through – they're in the den.'

'Thanks, Mrs Conway.'

The hallway was one of those ones where the upstairs landing was a balcony that went right the way round, and there was a massive swooping staircase in front of me. I'd got used to it by now, but it was still pretty impressive. Zack's mum disappeared back upstairs. 'Help yourself to whatever you want, love,' she called back to me. 'I've just got to put my face on.'

I wandered through the house, my footsteps echoing on the polished floorboards. The den was a room right at the back, looking out over the huge garden. It was kitted out with giant leather sofas, a wall-mounted flat-screen TV the size of a cinema screen, and a log fire. The house had this fancy sound system with hidden speakers in every room and a voice-activated dock, and in the den it was currently playing the playlist Zack had made for Malia. I recognised a couple of songs from the boat and felt sick.

'Logan!' Zack came towards me with a beer and did the Zack handshake. Dev was already sprawled on one sofa and

Marcus was sitting in one of the La-Z-Boy recliners. He raised his bottle to me in a toast.

I took the beer from Zack and downed most of it in one.

'Why didn't you invite JB?' I asked, before I even realised I was going to.

Zack frowned. 'Don't know what you're on about, mate.'

'Yes, you do. He was right there, next to me and Dev, and you blanked him. Just like you cut him out of the new WhatsApp group.'

Zack shrugged. 'Look, I know what you're thinking. But it's not personal, Lo. JB can do whatever the hell he wants with whoever he wants.'

'So why don't you want to hang round with him any more?' My voice was getting louder. I finished the rest of the beer.

Zack glanced back at Marcus and Dev, who were sitting there in silence, watching us. 'No offence, lads,' he said, looking from them to me and back again, 'but I can't have anyone thinking I'm some kind of faggot.'

I felt winded at the way the word just fell out of his mouth, like it was nothing. And I realised that it *had* been nothing – at school people called each other *gay* and *fag* and *homo* all the time, like it was funny. How had it taken me this long to realise that it wasn't?

'Who's a faggot?' Gordon said, appearing through the doorway with bags of takeaway. 'No son of mine, that's for sure.' He grinned at me. 'Hi, Logan. Let me get you another beer.'

I stared at Zack, and then I put my empty bottle down on the coffee table. 'That's OK, Mr Conway,' I said. 'Turns out, I'm not really in the mood for celebrating after all.'

I TOLD MUM I'd come home early because I was feeling ill. I went to bed and I mostly stayed there for the next week and mostly she let me. I told Daisy I was ill too and she sent me nice messages and funny links and she stayed away like I'd asked her to.

I didn't tell Zack anything because I didn't bother replying to his messages. I left the new WhatsApp group and I put the old one on mute. After a while, I realised my phone had an off button and I pressed it, and some days it stayed off.

I stopped sleeping at night at all really. I would lie there and lie there and I'd think, *Soon I should go to sleep*, but just the act of turning over, of closing my eyes, felt impossible. And so I'd stay where I was, letting all these thoughts keep circling through my head. *I should've studied more. I thought I was so smart. I'm an idiot. I'll have to completely rethink my UCAS application. Maybe I shouldn't even bother going to uni. I probably can't hack it anyway, look at me.*

It went on like that for hours sometimes, while I just lay looking at the ceiling. I kept thinking of Uncle Darius's face on my phone screen. *Good man. Yeah, right,* the voice inside my head kept saying. *Can't even get a job in a sandwich bar, can't even get the marks I was predicted in piss-easy AS exams. Why would Daisy even want to be with me? She could do so much better.*

Sometimes I felt like crying but mostly I just lay still, because doing anything more would have felt like moving a mountain. The voice liked that too.

What do I have to cry about? What's actually wrong with me? Man up.

Man up man up man UP.

Loser.

Maybe you're thinking the same.

One night, lying there, I ended up on Facebook. I'd had an account since Year 9 but I hardly ever used it any more – I'd kind of stopped when me and Hope were together, because she wasn't on it and thought it was kind of lame. Getting the friend request from Lucy was the only reason I'd opened the app in weeks. But, you know, there's only so much stuff to look at on the Internet and I was bored of my usual sites, so I logged in to see what was going on.

It was mostly the same old thing – people posting memes I'd seen a million times and funny cat videos which, to be fair, I always appreciated. Charlotte had posted some photos of her, Daisy and Georgie in the park, and it was kind of nice to see those. Nice to see Daisy happy.

Better off without me, the voice said as I carried on scrolling down.

I was surprised to see Nate's name crop up in my feed. I didn't even know he still uploaded stuff to Facebook. But he'd posted a whole album of photos, 'Malia 17', only a couple of hours before. I clicked on the first picture, the six of us at the airport, taken by the minibus driver we'd hired. It'd been an early start and Zack's parents had said they'd rather pay for that than get up and take us. It'd been so much more exciting, all of us bundled into a seven-seater, the sky getting lighter as we bombed along the motorway, and the driver had let Zack hook his phone up to the stereo. We'd ended up chatting to him, this young guy, and when we'd all lugged our bags out onto the pavement outside Departures, he'd offered to get a photo of us. I studied us all, arms round each other, grinning and looking half asleep, half drunk already. It seemed like a long time ago.

I flicked through the rest of the album – mostly group shots, a couple of JB throwing up and one of Dev asleep standing up in a bar somewhere, his head resting against the sweaty wall. There was a cool one of me, Zack and JB jumping into the pool one afternoon, where Nate had caught us mid-air, and another good one of him and Hope on loungers, both wearing shades and making fake-pouty faces. A shot of all of us outside Rodeo, the first or second night, all of us laughing at something someone must have said just before Nate took the picture, and the lights flashing bright pink behind us so we all kind of glowed. I liked that one. I downloaded it, thought about making it my desktop background.

We all look so close, I thought. Surely we can be again?

Admittedly I'd started in on a bottle of rum from Mum's cupboard.

There was a photo of Dev and Hope dancing on the boat, a crowd gathering round them. I didn't remember that happening, and my stomach lurched, searching the crowd for the guy in the vest top. I didn't know if I was ready to see his face again.

The next photos were on the boat too, but they weren't particularly good – a selfie Nate had taken with JB, where the angle was bad and it was mostly their foreheads with a bit of sea behind them. One of the crowd on the deck which was kind of blurry, like Nate's hand had moved while he was taking it. And then one on the island, at night, when the paint party was happening – but Nate hadn't used his flash so it was mostly dark, you could only make out the DJ with his strobe light.

I was clicking through fast, not even sure why I was still going. I didn't want to see any photos of myself that night. I didn't want to remember it any more.

But I was in luck, because there weren't any photos of me. That was maybe a bit weird, given me and Nate had ended up spending most of the day together – but then I guessed it hadn't really been a photo-taking kind of time. It had all started with him asking me about what had happened with Hope the night before – I guess she'd told him about it after I'd left. We'd both been wasted and we'd ended up talking for a long time, just sitting on a couple of big rocks on the other side of the woods, away from the party.

And then everything had just started spilling out – I'd even started trying to explain how I'd felt after me and Hope broke up, how I'd already been feeling down before that happened, and even though I wasn't exactly in the right state for a heart-to-heart, Nate had actually listened. I'd told him how me and Daisy had been arguing, how guilty I was feeling about the whole Hope thing, and he'd understood.

'It'll all sort itself out,' he'd said. 'You can talk to me, you know.'

I'd really believed it then – and we'd ended up talking about all kinds of crap, drunk with our bare feet hanging in the sea: about my dad living in America and Nate's parents putting pressure on him to go to uni, about how Daisy and me were kind of different and it worried me, about how Nate had never really liked anyone as much as he liked Polly. About how much he missed his sister, who'd died two years ago.

It had felt great, opening up like that, but we'd been drunk. I tried to imagine calling him up now and telling him how much worse I was feeling, but I couldn't. What was he supposed to say? Um, get some real problems, Logan?

I glanced at the next photo. It was in a bar somewhere, so I assumed it was the next night. The last night. But I wasn't in this one either – it was just Zack, Nate and Dev. I stared at it for a second, wondering what was bothering me about it.

And then my eye caught on Dev's vest. It was the same one he'd been wearing on the boat.

I mean, I'm not the kind of guy that pays much attention to his mates' clothes. But, like most of Dev's clothes, this was a pretty distinctive vest.

I flicked back to the boat pictures and then forward to the bar one. All three of them, same clothes. Nate had taken the picture himself – you could see his forearm along the right side of the picture, and they were all cheering into the camera, their eyes bloodshot and glazed-looking. They certainly looked like they'd been on it all day.

This was definitely the night of the boat party. The night Zack had come home with me, and I assumed he'd fallen asleep in the same room I had.

183

So what was he doing out on the strip with those two?

And why had they all lied about it?

I clicked onto the next picture in the album. Same night, same outfits, same bar – but in this one it was Zack and Dev, both with their heads tilted back as they tried to down a pint of something, whatever it was splashing all over both of them and the floor. Nate's thumb obscured the bottom left corner of the screen, and above it you could just make out a group of guys clapping Zack and Dev. I switched my attention to the other side of the photo, which was mostly taken up by the bar – industrial-looking metal with green lights hanging over it.

But right at the edge of the photo, the bottom right corner, there was something else.

At first I thought it was just Nate's other thumb. He'd been drunk enough that it was pretty likely. But when I looked closer, I realised that it was someone's hair – someone standing in front of Nate, *right* in front of Nate, and just in the edge of the shot. Someone with reddish blonde hair.

Emily had reddish blonde hair.

Emily had told her friends she was going to the strip.

Emily had gone *missing*.

My friends had lied about where they were when it happened.

My heart beating fast, I clicked onto the next photo. But it was of the four of us in the Red Lion on the last day, and I remembered Lucy taking it.

And that was the last photo in the album. I flicked back to the two from that night, really searching them this time. *Was* that even the same colour hair as Emily's? I opened the article I'd found about her going missing and tried to look at

184

them side by side. It could have been her hair – but then it wasn't as if it was a particularly unusual colour, not like blue or something really recognisable.

Hardly damning evidence, I tried to tell myself. *Isn't it more likely they just lied because they wanted a night out without you?*

I closed my laptop and lay there until it got light.

I DID TRY. Know that, if nothing else. The next morning, I pulled out my trainers and I jogged down to the park and I tried to feel something. Anything. My brain knew that the sun was on my face and the music was pounding in my ears, but it all felt so distant, like it was happening to someone else. When I got home, I stood in the shower and let the water wash over me for a long time.

Back in my room, my phone was ringing. Steph.

'Hey.'

'Hey, cuz,' I could hear her heels clicking along the pavement. 'Just on my lunch, thought I'd give you a call. Wanted to congratulate you on your results.'

My stomach twisted. 'Oh. Thanks.'

'Well, you sound happy about it. What's up – secretly hoping for four As?'

I tried to brighten my voice. 'Nah, just tired.'

'Out celebrating all week?'

'Yeah, something like that.' I sank down on the edge of the bed. 'How are you, anyway?'

'Ummm.' I heard the beeping of a pedestrian crossing, her footsteps speeding up. 'Yeah, I'm good. Knackered. But fine.'

'Uncle D taking the pottery world by storm yet?'

'Not exactly. He's still trying to master the humble plate. The garden looks kind of like an archaeologist has uncovered the remains of a Roman dinner party or something.'

I laughed. It felt strange.

'Hey,' she said. 'I saw something on Twitter yesterday about Malia.'

The knots in my stomach tightened. 'Oh yeah?'

'Yeah, someone had retweeted something about a missing girl who was there in July. Kind of creepy, huh?'

'Yeah, that's horrible,' I said.

'Apparently she just went out one night and then didn't show up at her hotel. No sign of her since.'

'Wow.' I didn't know what else to say.

'It really sucks being a girl, cuz,' she said. 'I'm telling you, half the time it feels like you're always one step away from being a missing poster or an obituary.'

I wondered what Steph would think of the way we'd all abandoned Hope on the beach. I didn't have to wonder very hard.

'OK, I've gotta head back into work,' she said, interrupting that thought. 'Speak soon, yeah?'

'Yeah. Have a good day.'

I was about to hang up when she said, 'Logan?'

'Yeah?'

'You sure you're all right?'

I was really glad that this was just a regular call, no FaceTime. 'Yeah,' I said, and I managed to lift my voice enough for it to sound convincing.

After I hung up, I opened Facebook and went straight to

Nate's profile. The album was at the top of his page and I opened it, searching through the thumbnails to find the photo again.

I blinked, checked again. I clicked on the last photo – the one of the four of us in the Red Lion, and then went backwards, to where the photo had been the day before. But the previous one in the album was the one on the beach at the island.

I went backwards and forwards through every photo three or four times. But I wasn't imagining it – those two photos of the three of them that night had disappeared. They'd been deleted.

A COUPLE OF days later, I couldn't pretend I was ill any more, not to Mum or Daisy. So when Daisy asked if I wanted to meet at the park, I said yes. I was just finishing getting dressed when my phone buzzed with a message from Dev.

Dude check this out!

There was a link pasted in and he'd followed it with a laughing emoji and a shocked one. I clicked and it took me through to a TV channel's website, to their catch-up player. I scrolled down to the programme title. *Sun, Sand and Secrets on Tour: Malia*.

I flipped open my laptop and opened the website on there instead, so that I could see it properly.

In the final episode of the series, the Sun, Sand and Secrets *team hit the Greek island of Crete to check out legendary party destination Malia. We follow a group of young thrill-seekers as the fishbowls flow . . . but what happens on tour doesn't always stay on tour . . .*

I picked up my phone and messaged Dev back.

Are we on this?

Mate watch it!

I reached out and clicked play on my laptop, my stomach churning. I hadn't seen any cameras filming us, I tried to reason with myself. It wasn't as if a camera crew could have followed Zack and me down that alley – and even if they *had*, Dev would hardly have sent it to me with a laughing face.

Would he?

'Tonight on *Sun, Sand and Secrets* . . .' the voiceover woman was saying. She had a friendly, familiar Scottish accent – she was off a soap or something, but I couldn't concentrate enough to remember which one. I was too busy watching the clips they were playing. Packed bars and people cheering at the camera, a girl standing in the middle of the strip downing a fishbowl while half of it spilled over her. Two boys fighting outside a bar – my heart dropped in my chest, but it wasn't us – and then a couple snogging up against a police car.

It made me feel wrong. Anxious, hungover – like my brain was remembering all of the bad stuff and none of the good. They showed a clip of someone throwing up on the road, and I thought I was going to heave too.

When the programme started properly, it introduced two sets of friends – two boys from Newcastle and a group of four girls from London. I didn't recognise any of them and my stomach started to settle, just a bit. The screen showed both groups getting ready for their first night out and then them venturing onto the strip, and their excitement started to bring back some of the good feeling I'd had on *our* first night. I remembered what it was like, taking in all the colours and the lights and the music, this feeling like all the adults had gone away and left us kids to play. Rides and shots and glow sticks and everyone trying to get your attention, everyone trying to help you have a good time.

I got so lost in the memory of it that I even started looking for us whenever they showed footage of a bar or club or crowded bits of the strip. I started looking out for anyone I recognised – and then I remembered Emily, and the good feeling went away.

The girls got up on the bar in one place and started dancing, people passing them shot after shot. One of them fell off and twisted her ankle, and the camera crew followed them as one of her friends give her a piggyback to the 24-hour walk-in clinic right in the middle of the strip. The resigned-looking guy there bandaged it up and took her insurance details, while her mates sat outside eating chips.

They cut to the guys then, who were hanging around a bar and trying to get chatting to girls – any girls; they didn't seem that picky. 'He's gonna watch and learn,' one of them said to the camera, looking hammered already and pointing to his mate, 'because tonight I'm gonna show him how to take the trash out.'

I tapped the trackpad to see how much of the programme was left – I was almost halfway through and there was no sign of any of us. Maybe Dev had just sent it because it had given him that happy first-night feeling too. Maybe he just wanted me to remember how we'd all been instead of focusing on the mess we were in now.

But then I saw Nate. The edge of his face, just passing the

camera as it filmed the two guys throwing some dodgy shapes on the dance floor.

It was enough though. I knew that this was the same week. I knew that we were there too.

I didn't have to wait long. After a couple of clips of the groups hungover on the beach and of one of the girls panicking that she'd lost her passport, there was another night out.

I recognised the bar right away. Rodeo. My eyes kept trying to go to the part of the room we'd been in, but the camera was facing the wrong way. It was an agonising couple of minutes before one of the girls persuaded another that they should go on the buckin' bronco and the camera panned through the crowd to follow them.

And there we were. All of us, with our two fishbowls, bouncing a bit to the music and watching people around us. We were drunk, I could tell, although we weren't doing anything embarrassing. JB leaned in to say something to Dev, arm round him, and I turned to Nate, and then, just like that, the camera was past us and we were gone.

I dragged the slider back and watched the scene again. Hope laughing at something with Zack, Dev going in for another swig of fishbowl before JB leaned in to tell him whatever it was he was telling him.

I watched it again. I don't know what I was looking for.

Even though I'd been afraid before, now I couldn't stop looking for us, *wanting* to see us. I wanted to climb back through that screen and into my body – to tell JB not to be scared about telling us who he liked and who he didn't, and to make Zack understand that it wasn't a big deal. I wanted to grab Dev by the face and tell him that it was OK to still miss Mollie, that he didn't have to prove anything by pulling anyone who'd have him. And Hope . . . I wanted to tell Hope how good it was that we were mates. I wanted to stop myself flirting with her just because me and Daisy had had a stupid row, because Hope deserved better than that.

But all I could do was watch.

Watch and rewatch and wonder.

The two Geordie boys made friends with a group from Liverpool and rented mopeds. I was surprised Zack hadn't thought of that. They were shown driving down the strip just as the sun was setting, whooping and revving their engines as the lights stuttered on and the chairs were set out.

The show cut back to the girls, the voiceover lady explaining that the missing passport had been found and everything was OK. They were getting ready for their last night out and I tensed, wondering where it'd be. Where *we* would be. What if they'd managed to film me and Hope sitting out on the steps? Would it look bad?

But the girls were in a club I didn't recognise, and when they cut to the boys, they were in Guys and Dolls, the massive super-club which cost twenty euros to get into and which we'd heard was crap.

I checked the scrub bar – only a couple of minutes left of the episode. One of the girls was being sick outside while another held her hair back and the others sang a Rihanna song. And the boys were celebrating one of them getting off with one of the Liverpudlian girls that he liked by buying kebabs.

'And so another night on the strip draws to a close,' the

voiceover woman said. 'And it looks like not everyone's had such a great time . . .'

There were more clips of people being sick and the two boys they'd shown in the introduction fighting, plus a girl crying on the steps of a club, her make-up running down her face. And then a girl lying . . .

A girl lying on the beach.

Alone.

Skirt up round her waist.

My hand was shaking as I scrolled back a couple of seconds and watched again. I had to pause it – it was only a split second of footage, before they moved on to three guys pissing up against a McDonalds – but I knew it was her. Her face was turned away from the camera but it was her. It was Hope.

They'd filmed her and they'd left her there.

I slammed the lid of my laptop down and grabbed my phone.

'You think that's funny?' I yelled, when Dev answered. 'That was *your* fault!'

'Huh?' Through my rage I registered that Dev sounded genuinely bewildered. 'Logan, what are you talking about?'

'Hope,' I said, through gritted teeth. 'You think it's a joke now?'

'No, of course not, mate. I just thought it was cool, seeing us all on telly, all of us getting on, you know –'

'You thought it was *cool* to see our friend passed the fuck out where we all left her – on some TV show where the whole world can also see it?'

There was a silence. 'Logan, I have no idea what you're talking about.'

'At the end! Right at the end! They filmed her! On that night. On the beach.'

'What?!' I could hear him typing something in the background, and then I heard the theme music of the show. 'Oh my God. I didn't see that, Logan, I swear. I just saw the six of us in Rodeo.'

'Yeah, well, watch it to the end,' I said, and I hung up on him.

I was going to be late to meet Daisy, but I couldn't stop myself opening the laptop again. It felt wrong watching the footage – I knew Hope wouldn't want me to, and I wondered if I should even tell her it existed. That someone had not only seen her there, all on her own, but had switched on their camera and filmed her.

I grabbed my phone and left, just as Dev sent me a message.

```
Shit. That's messed up. I didn't see it
1st time, I swear
```

I didn't bother replying.

I couldn't trust him. Any of them. And Emily Simpson was still missing.

I ACTUALLY GOT to the park before Daisy. The sun had disappeared behind a massive cloud, but it was warm enough for people to be out in force, so most of the scrappy grass was colonised already. I found a spot near the duck pond and texted Daisy to tell her.

'Hey,' she said, a few minutes later, dropping her bag and flopping down beside it. 'Sorry, I had to wait for Mum's birthday present to be delivered. I missed it the other day and they took it to the sorting office in frigging Huntstable.'

'No worries,' I said, and then I leaned over, realising we hadn't kissed yet.

'So,' she said, after pecking me, 'you feeling better?'

'Yeah.' I couldn't quite meet her eye. 'I missed you.'

She smiled. 'Good. About feeling better, I mean. Missing me is a bonus though.' She reached for her bag. 'Hey, I brought processed meat products.'

I laughed and took a Peperami. 'I do love my processed meat.'

'I know! I'm such a good girlfriend.' She tossed a chicken bite into her mouth and grinned at me, and even though the sun was still stubbornly behind a cloud, I felt the truth dawn on me all over again. I would never be good enough for her. I would never be the person she deserved. I was a guy who beat

196

up other guys in alleyways, two against one. I was a guy who left his friend – his ex-girlfriend – passed out on a beach. I was a guy who spent whole days and whole nights in bed because I couldn't bring myself to even swing one leg out and onto the floor. I was a guy who couldn't even get a job in a shitty sandwich place or collecting glasses in a bar. Daisy deserved more and she always would.

'Logan?' Daisy was looking over the top of her sunglasses – round, John Lennon-style ones today, that she'd found in the charity shop in town – at me. 'You OK?'

I swallowed, trying to push the thought away. 'Yeah. Sorry. Not sure I was quite ready for Peperami action just yet.'

'You're not gonna puke on me, are you?'

'Ha! No, you're safe for now.'

I slid my own sunglasses on because that felt better. Daisy knew me too well; she could see that I was hiding something. A tiny, hopeful voice inside me was pushing me to tell her how I'd been feeling. But that meant trying to explain, and I didn't know how. The word knot was there again, and untangling the words and getting them in the right order seemed impossible.

And so instead I asked, 'How's the book?'

She made an 'Eek' face. 'I finished it.'

'Wow! Daisy, that's great!'

'Thank you.' She hooked the hairband from round her wrist and twisted her hair up into a knot thing. 'It took a few all-night editing sessions, but I'm really happy with it.'

'It's amazing. That's such an achievement.'

I was totally in awe of her, and it made me feel happy. I know that's going to sound like a lie, with what comes next, but it did.

'I'm working on a sequel,' she said. 'Well, by working on, I mean writing random things in a notebook.'

'You've got to give the people what they want,' I said.

She smiled. 'Yeah. Pretty nerve-wracking to be honest. I've had loads of comments already from people saying what they want in the sequel. I don't want to let any of them down.'

'You won't. Seriously, Daisy. You know this story. You're the only one who can tell it.'

She slid her sunglasses down and looked over them at me again. 'You liked it then?'

I hadn't read it.

And I hate myself just as much for that, trust me.

'I love it,' I said. 'But I haven't finished yet, so no spoilers.'

I thought I saw a flicker of disappointment on her face and it felt like a knife in my gut.

I'd wanted to read it, I really had. So many times I'd picked up the laptop and started, but I just couldn't get the words to go into my brain. I'd spend hours focusing on them, trying to concentrate, but then I'd end up looking at tumblr or comics instead. That's how stupid I was. Only pictures for the idiot in his bedroom.

Daisy lay back on the grass, hands resting on her belly. 'Did you talk to Zack? What he did to JB on results day was so unbelievably unacceptable.'

'Yeah,' I said. 'I talked to him.' I wanted to add, *And I'm not talking to him any more*, but it seemed so childish, so completely avoiding the problem, that I couldn't bring myself to say it.

'Good.' She reached out and stuck her hand in the chicken-bites packet. 'It's got to come from your friends, I think. If your friends can't tell you you're an absolute asshat, who can?'

'Yeah.' I rolled onto my side and picked at the grass.

Daisy was looking at her phone. She frowned. 'Charlotte just sent me a link.'

I looked up. 'A link to what?'

She didn't answer, because she was slipping her earbuds into her ears. Even though the sun had finally crept from behind its cloud, I felt cold. I had a good idea what she was looking at.

'Hey, this is you!' she said, and my heart sank. Daisy got up and sat next to me to show me the phone, and I expected to see that same couple of seconds of footage of all of us in Rodeo.

But I'd never seen this clip before.

It was me and Nate, arms round each other, singing, both of us with a bottle in hand, and we were looking right at the camera.

'I don't remember that,' I said. 'Can I see?'

'Sure.' Daisy handed me the phone, tugging her earphones out.

I looked at the screen. It wasn't the catch-up player I was expecting, but a YouTube clip. I scrolled down to look at the details. '*Sun, Sand and Secrets . . . the Unseen Footage!*'

I couldn't watch it. Not with Daisy there, looking at me. So I just said, 'Oh, Dev sent me this earlier. We're only in that little bit. We look absolutely battered.'

'Oh. Boring.'

I closed the window and handed her back her phone. Then I lay back on the grass so I wouldn't have to see her watching me. After a minute, she lay down too.

We didn't speak much after that. All I could think about were the endless reasons why Daisy would be better off without me.

I want to be the kind of guy who took those feelings and said, *Well, then I need to be better*.

I want to be the guy who can say, *And so I promised myself I would work as hard as I could from then on to be the person she deserved*.

At the very least, I want to be the guy who spoke to her there and then and told her what was on my mind.

I'm none of those things. I broke up with her that night. By text.

Do you hate me now?

I DIDN'T EVEN have to make excuses after that. Mum had to go on a training course for a week, and I got myself into a comfortable routine of one takeaway a day, sixteen hours' sleep and eight or so hours of self-loathing.

I watched the YouTube footage of us most days. It had been taken on the beach, the boat in the background, and everyone was a mess. People leering and lunging at the camera, people clinging to each other and laughing, singing, hanging on as tight as they could. There was hardly any light, and if you watched it with the sound off, it looked a bit like found footage from the end of the world. It looked like we had all survived a terrible event, like we were all traumatised and afraid – until you turned on the sound and heard the muddled lyrics and the shouted jokes and the constant cheering and wolf-howling.

Nate was gone, anyone could see that. He was leaning into me, his eyes half closed, his mouth not quite keeping up with the lines he was trying to sing.

But me? I looked all right. I couldn't remember being filmed but I didn't look out of control. I didn't look like a person who wasn't responsible for his actions.

I recognised some other people from the boat – the couple

who'd won the sex positions were there, him giving her a piggyback across the sand.

And then, with a group of guys, there was Hope. They were singing Bon Jovi, randomly, and Hope's eyes kept rolling up behind her eyelids. The boys were jumping around and she was bumbling against them, as if half the time she didn't even know they were there, and then, just before the clip ended, she staggered away from them and out of shot.

I wanted, more than anything, to reach in and grab hold of the camera and turn it to follow her, to see who was out of the frame, to search for any of us and drag us over there to help her. To drag *all* of us together and send us off in the direction of burgers and home.

But obviously I couldn't. So I just lay there and watched.

I looked for Emily. Of course I did. Every shot, every second of that film, I looked for her. I dreaded seeing Zack with his arm round her or Nate leaning in to whisper to her. I didn't want to see anything that might make me have to drag those niggling thoughts out of the darkest corner of my head and into the light.

And I was lucky, or they were. Because Emily didn't show up in a single scene. It was like she'd never been there at all.

Steph had got into the habit of calling me on her way to work, reporting back as Uncle Darius made his way up from plates to bowls and one not-very-vaseish vase. I liked her calls because she talked so much they didn't require much input from me, and it was comforting to hear her voice.

But after a couple of days she started asking me what I was up to. I'd make excuses at first – say I was waiting in for a delivery or that I was hungover. After a while though, she didn't let things slide so easily.

'Are you doing anything today? You should step outside, cuz, it's a beautiful day. You know, get some fresh air.'

'Fresh air's overrated.' It came out harsher than I meant it to.

'Well. You know. It's actually not raining here for once.'

I couldn't think of anything to say. That was happening more often – I've never been good at small talk, but without practice my skills were disappearing entirely. That was why talking to Steph usually felt OK – she didn't really require it.

'Hey,' she said, 'you could come and visit. If you're not up to much. Come see us, make yourself a new plate. It'll be wild.'

The prospect of being in their loud, lime-green-and-peach kitchen did appeal, suddenly. To be around their noise and the constant food and the ease of being with people who've known you your whole life.

But then I thought about getting the train, and getting a taxi from the train, and of talking about how I was and results and what my plans were, and I just wanted to close my eyes and not open them for a while. I thought about how much it cost to get a train to Manchester and about the fact that I'd spent all of my savings on the holiday and now had no way of getting any more.

'I can't,' I said. 'No cash at the moment. Soon though.'

'Well, I could buy your ticket,' she said. 'Stupid shoe money is starting to build up, especially when Mum and Dad refuse to charge me any rent.'

It was so kind and she said it so easily, like it was no big deal, that it made me want to cry and it made me feel even worse.

'Nah, I can't let you do that,' I said, and my voice sounded thin and feeble. 'When Mum gets back I'll talk to her – I bet she'd love to drive up one weekend.'

I believed it too. I really thought, in a week or a month, that'll be great. I just need a couple of days to myself, that's all.

I really thought, they're my friends. I should trust them.

It's amazing, the lies you can tell yourself.

IT TURNED OUT to be harder to lie to other people. Especially people as persistent as Steph.

The next day she didn't call on her way to work or on her lunch. I didn't realise I'd missed speaking to her until an hour later, when the word knot felt particularly heavy and I kept having to take a deep breath on purpose, because all of a sudden it felt like I couldn't breathe.

But then she *did* call, right when things felt so bad – like I was standing looking into a deep, dark hole with no way back from it – that I'd been wondering if I should call 999. *And say what?* the voice in my head sneered. *I feel so sad it's like I'm actually suffocating?*

It was after lunchtime and Steph wasn't walking anywhere. She was sitting somewhere quiet and her voice was quiet too when she said: 'I'm worried about you.'

'Why? I'm fine?'

But I wasn't fine. I was crying.

'Logan, I think you've got depression.'

I didn't tell her I'd been googling it myself, reading the symptoms over and over. I couldn't say it out loud. 'Don't be stupid,' I said instead, drawing a shaky breath and pushing the tears off my face with a fist. 'What have I got to be depressed about?'

205

She tutted. 'It doesn't work like that. It's an illness. Have you told any of your friends how you're feeling? Zack or Dev or JB?'

I laughed and was shocked at how bitter it came out. 'I can't do that. We don't talk about stuff like that.'

'Why not? You guys have known each other since you were kids.'

'Yeah, but . . . We just don't. It'd be weird.'

'What you're saying is weird. You realise that, right? You're basically saying you can't tell your best friends about something really bad that you're feeling.'

I sighed and lay back. This conversation felt exhausting. 'That's just how it is with blokes. We didn't even talk about it when Nate's sister died.'

'No, Logan, that's not "just how it is".' Steph sounded angry. 'Don't pull this "man up" bullshit with me. Friends are friends, whatever gender they are. If you're hurting, you tell them. Try them – I think you'd be surprised.'

I had to swallow a couple of times before I could coax the words out. 'I'm embarrassed,' I said, and my voice was very small.

There was a silence and I thought it was because Steph was embarrassed too. But when she spoke, I realised she was crying. 'Do *not* be embarrassed about this,' she said. 'Promise me. You have nothing to be embarrassed about.'

'OK,' I said, and then we were both quiet.

'Look, just think about it, OK?' she said, clearing her throat. 'Or talk to someone else, someone you don't know if that feels easier. There's loads of help you can get. You don't have to feel ashamed.'

I looked away, concentrating on a cobweb in the corner of the ceiling. 'I better go,' I said.

'OK.' She was quiet for a second. 'Look, I'm always here, OK. You can talk to me, even if you won't talk to anyone else.'

'I know,' I said, and my voice cracked. 'Thanks.'

I hung up as quickly as I could. And then I lay down and closed my eyes and listened to the voice in my head telling me over and over how pathetic I was.

TALKING TO STEPH had helped somehow. It had definitely kick-started *something* in my head, anyway, because that night when I couldn't sleep, I didn't just lie there. I got up and went to make myself a cup of tea.

I took it back to my room and sat at my little desk with it for a while. I wasn't exactly full of beans, but moving a limb didn't seem like lifting steel either, and I looked around my room and wondered if tidying it might help things a bit. There were plates stacked around my bed and I was getting a good stockpile of empty bottles there too – I didn't look at them for too long, because they made me feel guilty and sick. What kind of person drinks themselves to sleep at seventeen?

I shifted my attention to the rest of the room. My desk chair had clothes thrown over the back of it – clean or dirty, I couldn't remember. And by the narrow wardrobe was my holdall from Malia, which I still hadn't got round to unpacking despite Mum bringing it up every other day.

Even I could admit that that was pretty disgusting, and sorting it out felt like an achievable task. So I scooted my chair over and lifted the bag into my lap. Most things could just go straight into the wash-basket, where I could tackle them tomorrow. Maybe. This was already beginning to feel like an effort.

I started taking things out and throwing them into a pile. Paint-splashed T-shirts and a pair of shorts with a sticky cocktail stain. Then I remembered Mum's golden rule of laundry: *Always check the pockets.* There had been one or two – or twenty – times when I'd ruined a new jumper or whatever of hers by leaving a receipt or a tissue in my jeans. I pulled out the next pair of shorts and checked its pockets – all clear. Another T-shirt and a couple of pairs of boxers went on the pile, and then out came the plastic bag with my shampoo and shower gel in them. I dumped that on the desk – it looked like one of the bottles had leaked, but I wasn't sure I was ready to tackle that just yet – and kept going.

Flip-flops went straight into the wardrobe, a little shower of sand going with them. Already I felt pleased with myself, more so than I had for weeks. I realise how ridiculous that sounds. But somehow I felt like if I could get to the bottom of this bag, put everything where it should be and pack the bag away into the top of my wardrobe, I'd have taken a step. Even if it was just a baby one.

At the bottom there was one last pair of shorts – beige-coloured chino-type ones. I frowned, looking at them, and then at the pile on the floor, where a very similar-looking pair were already tangled up. These ones were heavier, made of a posher material, and they had a print of palm trees on the inside. They weren't mine – I must have picked them up in the rush to pack.

I thought back, mentally flicking through images of the

holiday, and my brain landed on one very clear one. Me and Nate, sitting on the rock, our feet dipped in the sea. Nate in his white T-shirt and the shorts I was now holding in my hand.

I folded them, about to add them to the pile so that I could at least return them to him washed, when I remembered the pockets rule.

The back pockets were empty except for a couple of loose coins, and so was the left – but in the right pocket my fingers hit paper. I pulled it out and found a five-euro note, crumpled up, and inside it, a receipt.

Turning back to the desk, I smoothed it out. The receipt itself was mostly in Greek, but the price was there – €25. Probably for a round, I supposed. Probably from the bar the three of them somehow ended up at, the bar I was trying not to think about.

I was about to screw it up and chuck it, when I saw the logo at the top of the receipt. It was big and smudged so I hadn't paid much attention to it at first – but when I looked again, I saw that the words printed underneath were small but legible. And in English.

Popeye's Petrol Stop

I sat back in my chair, thinking. What had Nate bought from a petrol station for €25? I thought I could remember this Popeye's place, too – it had been right at the end of the strip, on the way to our hotel, where there weren't really any bars, just a couple of small restaurants and a phone-repair place. If it was the place I was thinking of, it hadn't even had a shop, just two petrol pumps. It was just a place where you bought petrol.

So what had Nate been doing buying petrol?

THE DOORBELL RANG early the next morning.

Well, I say early. It was 11 a.m., but by then that was early to me. I could easily sleep until two or three in the afternoon – and if I woke up, I just turned over and closed my eyes until I wasn't awake any more.

I lay there and hoped whoever it was would go away. If it was a parcel, the postman would leave it in the communal hallway like he always did – my presence was not required.

But the doorbell rang again. Longer and louder this time. I got out of bed and threw a hoodie on over my pyjama bottoms. Standing in my bedroom doorway, I tried to make out who was there through the panel of frosted glass in the front door, but all I could see was the top of a head. Blondish hair.

Not Daisy, the voice inside my head said, with satisfaction. *Why would it be?*

I walked down the hallway and opened the door.

It was Zack. 'All right, mate,' he said. 'Gonna invite me in or what?'

I followed him into the living room, where the curtains were still drawn. They probably had been since Mum had left, I couldn't remember. I pulled them open as Zack sank down on the sofa.

'Do you want a cup of tea?' I asked.

'Nah, you're all right.' He looked at me. 'You look like shit, Loges.'

'Yeah. I've – I've been ill.'

Zack nodded, still looking at me. 'I heard about you and Daisy splitting up. You OK?'

'Yeah.' I shrugged. 'It's shit, obviously.'

I was trying to hide my surprise. Even though Zack had always been there when one of us broke up with a girlfriend, it wasn't exactly like him to just show up at my house.

'Any chance of you guys working it out?' he asked. He was leaning back in his seat, arm spread across the back and legs stretched out.

'I don't know.' I sat down on the armchair opposite him. 'I really don't.'

'You missing her?'

'Yeah, course.' I could feel him watching me and I didn't want to meet his eye.

'So. Go make up with her.'

I shook my head. 'It's complicated.'

'Doesn't seem that complicated to me. You're moping round here like a wet weekend, when you should be going round there and sorting it out.'

I stayed silent. I wanted him to stop talking.

'Look, Logan, I'm getting some seriously bad vibes off you right now. And you threw that shit fit the other week too.'

A flash of anger travelled through me. 'Don't do that.'

212

'Do what?' He looked genuinely bewildered.

'Don't try and make out that I was having a *strop*. You know exactly why I was upset.'

Zack looked back at me, wide-eyed. 'I genuinely don't, mate.'

I looked away from him. 'You've been keeping things from me. All of you.'

'What are you on about?'

'That night,' I said. It came out in a growl. 'What happened? Tell me what the three of you did.'

'Lo. What are you on about?'

'Don't lie!' I stood up, realising my hands were shaking. 'The three of you went out that night and then you lied about it. You were out and you lied and a girl went missing.'

Zack had his hands out in his *calm down* way, like he was going to try to herd me back into my pen. 'A girl went missing? You're talking about that Emily chick?'

'Yes.' I made myself look him in the eye. 'What did you do?'

He stared right back at me.

And then he laughed.

'You cannot be serious. Logan Mitchell, as I live and breathe, accusing his best friends of . . . of what, Lo? Murder?'

I shrugged. 'Can you blame me? You lie about where you are that night – you buy *petrol* –'

'How do you know about that?' Zack asked sharply, and I thought, *Got you*.

'I found the receipt. So don't try and lie. Again.'

Zack rolled his eyes. 'All right, fine. You want to know what happened that night, Miss Marple? Take a seat. Let me fill you in on the kind of guys you're friends with.'

I sank back down into my chair, because the habit of listening to Zack was a hard one to break.

'Yeah, OK, we went out that night,' he said, leaning forward to rest his elbows on his knees. His eyes hadn't left mine. 'You were passed out and snoring, and I was still buzzing from the fight. So sue me. Then I get a call from Nate, off his tits and lost on the strip somewhere, says he can't remember how to get home.'

He paused to raise an eyebrow at me, like *You know how he is*. 'So I head back out, Uncle Zack to the rescue, but on my way out I run into Dev. He's acting all sheepish cos he's obviously blown his chance with Lucy like a total fanny, but I rope him into coming with me to get Nate. Nate's not exactly a small guy – I figured I could use the help keeping him upright.'

I stared at him. 'Right.'

'Anyway.' He straightened up again and leaned back, relaxing into it. 'When we get there, Nate's actually sorted himself out a bit. I don't know, coffee or drugs or Red Bull, *something* – someone's helped him out somewhere along the line, because he's just chilling outside some bar, perfectly happy and making sense.

'And you know, we figure, well, we're out now. We may as well make the most of it. So we have a couple of drinks, we're having a good time –'

'With Emily?' I asked, my voice flat.

Zack shook his head, his face creased like I was an idiot. 'Of course not. Logan, I swear, I can barely even remember the girl.'

I looked away.

214

'The petrol . . .' I said.

'I'm getting to it. So, yeah, we've had a couple of drinks and, well, it was a big day, right? We were all completely caned. So it's time to hit the sack, and we head off towards the hotel. Except – look, this part is kind of funny, but it's also kind of bad. I don't know how you're gonna take it.'

I looked back at him, feeling sick. I didn't say anything.

'Well, look, we see these two mopeds parked down the side of one of the restaurants. I don't know – some tourists left them there thinking they were safe, or they belonged to the owner or whatever. Dev happened to wander down there to have a slash, and he sees them.'

He looked at me, eyes wide again. 'I mean, it was just a laugh. The keys were right there, it was funny.'

'You stole them.'

'Well, yeah.'

'You took mopeds for a joyride in that state?'

Zack shrugged. 'Look, like I say, it was kind of bad. That's why we didn't *tell* you about it the next day. So you wouldn't get into any trouble if anyone asked. You know, if we'd been caught on CCTV or whatever.'

I swallowed. I couldn't really get my head round this, not when I'd spent so long suspecting something so much worse. 'What happened to the bikes?'

Zack laughed. 'Dev fucking stacked it into a parked car halfway up the road,' he said. 'That boy should never be allowed a licence, I'm telling you. He couldn't steer a fucking trolley.'

'And the other one?'

He shrugged. 'Nate took it back first thing that morning.

Turns out he even filled the petrol back up, according to you.'

I was silent, taking it all in. I'd got it so wrong.

Zack laughed again. 'I can't believe he did that. What a gay.'

'Don't do that,' I said. 'Don't use that word as an insult.'

Zack frowned. 'What, gay? Come on, Lo, it's just banter. Don't change the subject just because you feel like a tit for blowing this whole thing way out of proportion.'

'You can't just cut him out!' I yelled, surprising myself.

'Who, JB?' Zack shrugged. 'Why would he want to hang out with us now anyway?'

'Oh, what, because he doesn't want to shag girls, suddenly he won't want to hang around with his oldest friends?'

Zack shrugged again and looked back at me.

I was angry now, really angry. It felt like all the energy I'd been missing for weeks was suddenly flooding through me. 'Is that really all you think we are? Is that all friends are meant to talk about?'

I'd expected another shrug – I was ready to go in on him even harder – but Zack dropped his gaze to the floor. 'You don't understand, mate,' he said eventually. His voice sounded different to the way it normally did. He sounded like he really *wanted* me to understand. 'My dad, the lads at rugby . . . They'd think . . .' He trailed off.

'They'd think what? That you caught a dose of gay? Jesus, Zack, you sound like you just walked out of the 1950s. JB is our friend and he fancies guys and it's really not a big deal.'

Zack's face turned red, but after a minute his eyes narrowed. 'I don't see *you* hanging around with him though, do I?'

I hadn't been hanging around with anyone. I'd been lying

in a darkened room for weeks because I couldn't even face the postman most days. But I couldn't tell Zack that. And so I just stared back at him.

He took my silence to mean that I agreed. He often did that.

'See? You find it weird too. It's messed up the whole group, Lo.'

'No,' I said. 'It hasn't. No one else cares apart from you, Zack. And that's a problem you need to deal with.'

He laughed, and I knew I'd handled this wrong. No one criticised Zack; he didn't understand it.

'Yeah. I'm the one with the problem. I'm not the one sitting here accusing my best mates of murdering some random girl. I'm not the one sitting here in the state you are. It's lunchtime, Logan, and you're in your pyjamas, stinking like something out of a swamp. All because you're scared you're not enough of a man for your girlfriend.'

I felt like he'd punched me in the face.

'Well, it's true, isn't it?' he said, getting up. 'Why don't you think about that before you try and lecture me. You need to man up, Logan. You're a mess.' He moved to the door, shaking his head. Before he stepped into the hallway, he turned to look back at me.

'Seriously, it's pathetic. You need to sort yourself out. You need to *do* something.'

People say blackouts are convenient. People who've never had one think they're a lie – they think it's something you say when you've done something you regret. Like saying, 'I can't remember anything,' is some kind of magic wand you can wave to make it all OK again. A blank slate, a do-over. They think it's a kind of denial.

A way to put your head in the sand.

They don't know what it's like to lose a small piece of your life like that. A moment or a minute or an hour where you are no longer your own. A section of time that exists only then, that you can never revisit. You can't even pinpoint the moment you'd change, the thing you'd rather you hadn't said or done – because as far as your brain's concerned, you never did.

The rest of the world knows differently.

They remember.

DAISY

YOU WILL SAY that you don't deserve this.

You will say that what happened happened. You will say that you did nothing wrong.

Sometimes I wonder if you're right.

We are all a year older now. We are all grown up, about to leave school behind. We are all ready to leave you behind.

It seems a long time, doesn't it, since you guys came home from Malia? Seems a long time ago that all we had to worry about were AS results and whether Georgie and Charlotte could both be invited to a party. That summer and all its strangeness is past and far away, like it doesn't even belong to us any more.

You turned eighteen first; September, a week into Year 13.

A week after you did what you did.

But wait.

Rewind.

I REMEMBER, OFTEN, this one afternoon late last summer. It wasn't long before we were due to go back to school, and I'd been shopping online for stationery. It's something everyone has always laughed at me for, the excitement I can feel over an empty notebook, a new pack of highlighters. But it makes me happy – nothing makes me feel calmer than a sheaf of blank pages, the possibilities they hold. It sounds silly now, maybe. But it was a nice thing to be doing on a lazy Thursday with September just around the corner.

Something made me watch that footage again. The stupid link Charlotte had sent me. *Sun, Sand and Secrets: The Unseen Footage.* I saw you all there, saw all of you sun-singed and wild, set free. And I wondered.

I know you've always thought that the girls were stupid for cancelling their holiday. I was never really part of the plans – I don't know if I would have gone. It seems strange, now, to think of all those afternoons and phone calls and free periods spent listening to Charlotte complain about Georgie. About how she'd changed, how she'd lost herself, how she was twice as interested as Josh was and almost definitely going to get hurt.

Josh never did hurt Georgie, not as far as I know. They're

off to Sunderland Uni, both of them, with plans to share a flat in their second year.

It's funny how things turn out, don't you think?

I turned off the clip because it scared me – maybe you won't believe that. But then maybe you might. Instead I opened the file where I kept the notes for my novel and started working through what might happen next.

I don't think you've ever been interested in the stories I write, and that's OK. We all have our things, right? I've never really been able to explain why I write, why I can't *stop*. Charlotte laughed once, when I told her I was writing a novel. You're seventeen, she said. You need to get out more.

Well.

But yes, that afternoon – stationery and planning, still feeling park-lazy. And then the text.

```
So sorry to do this. I don't know what to
say. But I think we should stop seeing
each other. I think we're better apart.
```

I do wonder, sometimes, if that was the beginning.

THE DAY AFTER I got dumped, I cancelled my plans. Some people don't do that, right? They just carry on as normal, pick up the pieces and drink some drinks and be done. I can't. I couldn't do it when me and my first boyfriend, Alex, broke up in Year 11, and I couldn't do it this time, either. I needed time to decompress or something; time to just let it hurt.

And dumped by text? Yeah, ouch.

So I cancelled my plans with Charlotte and I sat in my room. Picture me in fast-forward – I'm lying in bed with the duvet over my head; I'm sitting on the floor with my phone on the carpet in front of me, willing myself not to call. I'm lying across the foot of my bed on my back, looking at the ceiling; I'm lying on the floor on my front watching Jessica Jones throw someone through a wall. I'm curled up in my desk chair, staring at my laptop screen; I'm leaning back with my slippers up on the desk, watching Buffy throw someone through a wall.

Girl, Wallowing. You get the idea.

Look, the truth is, I want to say that I brushed it off, pulled on my best hot pants and hit a dance floor somewhere. I want to say that I danced all night and laughed with my friends and didn't think a single thing about anything but whether I needed a new drink or a different song.

I want to say all that, but I promised myself I would tell the truth here, and so I will.

I wallowed.

Maybe I would've gone on wallowing, wondering. But the third day, my phone rang and I felt like answering. It was Georgie, suggesting I go over; not asking anything. And I thought: why not? I peeled my pyjamas off and got into the shower.

Georgie's house was full of noise, just how it always is. Her dad was in the kitchen, blitzing some kind of juice in the blender while classical music tried to compete from the radio. JB and his mum were in the living room, trying to stick glitter to some kind of plinth. The air was swirling with it and thick with paint fumes and the smell of baking – Georgie was making cupcakes again. She brought out a plate of them and we sat on the sofa and watched JB try to brush the glitter off his jeans.

'You guys really aren't helping me come out without the clichés,' he told his mum with a grin, and then picked up one of the cupcakes – neon yellow icing on lilac batter – and ate half of it in one bite. He flopped down onto the sofa next to me. 'How's it going, Dais?'

I smiled and picked at a bit of the icing on my own cake. I knew Georgie would've told him about the break-up, but I didn't know if I was ready to talk about it in front of them all. Georgie glanced at me, reading my mind. 'Shall I give you a hand with that, Dinah?' she asked, getting up to help her stepmum lug some of the leftover fibreboard out towards the back door.

'You doing OK?' JB asked, once they were gone.

227

I want to say that I was angry, that I told him how much it hurt. But I said I wouldn't lie. I shrugged. I said, 'I'm fine.' And then I asked the thing I really cared about: 'Is he doing OK?'

JB scrunched up his cake case and stared at it. 'I honestly don't think so. But I can't get him to talk to me or admit it.'

It came over me then, this crushing wave of feeling that I hadn't been expecting. It was failure. I felt like I'd failed. 'He's shutting us all out,' I said. 'I don't understand why.'

'I think he's going through some things,' JB said, unfurling the cake case and refolding it into a neat triangle. 'I guess we all are.'

'How are *you* doing?' I asked. I put my cake down on the table, mostly uneaten. I'm not sure you've ever *really* known me, but I think you'll still understand that this was deeply out of character.

JB's turn to shrug, that handsome, angled face turned down. 'I'm all right. Everyone's been great.'

'Not *everyone*.'

He glanced up at me and smiled a small, sad smile. 'Can't win 'em all, I guess.'

Georgie came back in then, brushing wood dust from her hands. 'You guys want to go up and watch crappy horror films?'

JB stood up. 'I'm gonna have to leave you to it. I said I'd help Nate with something.'

I followed him into the hall while Georgie went to put the kettle on for us again. 'Do you think I should call him?' I asked, as he shoved his feet into his trainers and patted his pockets in search of keys. 'Not to . . . you know. But just to check he's all right?'

228

He'd been about to leave, hand already on the door knob, but he came back over to me then and put his arms round me.

'We're gonna be OK, Dais,' he said, breath warm against my neck. 'All of us. I promise.'

I spent the afternoon snuggled on the couch in JB and Georgie's den, watching terrible B-movies and drinking endless cups of tea and feeling like maybe, somehow, JB was right. Maybe we'd all get back to normal somehow, whatever normal was now.

THINGS DID GET better, just a bit, during those days, that last week or two of summer. I was sad but I was OK – sometimes you can be both. Charlotte and I cycled all the way around the lake and drank beers at the tiny bit of beachy shore until the sun went down; cycled back laughing on wobbly wheels. Georgie and Josh took me to a gig, the band of some guy he knew through his sister, and we danced together and pretended the music was good and ate chips on the bus home. And I wrote too. The words found me, and it helped. This world I'd built welcomed me back and so I tried to lose myself in it. I still do. Sometimes I wonder if you have anything like that.

The first book was easier, maybe because I was writing just for me. It felt amazing when people started reading it, when I would check each morning to see the number of reads, with its little eye-shaped icon, tick slowly up. The first time someone commented on a chapter, I felt like my cheeks were about to burst, I was smiling so much. I remember it so well, lying on my bed, looking at it over and over.

kcinthecity: love this so much! can't wait to find out what happens next ☺

I uploaded the next chapter that night. I actually had almost all of the book written by then – it'd been on my laptop for a while, but I kept playing around with it, thinking of new stuff to add in or deciding I didn't like parts of it. I don't even know what had made me upload the first couple of chapters to StoryCity in the first place. I'd been a little bit drunk, after a party round at Charlotte's, and I'd been in bed reading but not really reading. I'd been thinking about it for a while, because I loved that site, loved reading some of the stories on there. But I hadn't had the nerve to share my own stuff. Well, booze gives you the nerve sometimes, right? You know that.

So I started editing the rest of the stuff I had, and uploading a new chapter every couple of days. kcinthecity commented every time, and I can't even explain how cool that felt, that someone was interested in Hannah, my main character, and all the weird stuff she was investigating.

But then when more people started reading, giving me stars and commenting too, I started to panic. I wasn't sure how the story was going to end – I'd thought for a while that Hannah might give up her investigating, that something might happen that meant she couldn't any more. But everyone seemed to love that stuff – they kept suggesting other paranormal things that might happen, or wondering if anyone would figure out that the famous author Hannah Hass was actually writing non-fiction in her novels. In Chapter Ten, Hannah met a vampire called Tobias and people really liked that bit. I started wondering if I should develop that more – I'd wanted them to become kind of friends but never *really* trust each other, but then kc and darkangel, another regular

231

reader, started debating whether they were going to end up together.

```
omg id love that sooooo much

it'd be so cool

he could join the business! dream team!
```

I started thinking maybe that *could* be quite cool. I even started writing a rough draft of a chapter where they kissed.

Then one evening, I checked the comments again. A new user, ryecatcher, had joined in the conversation.

```
omg no that would be such a Buffy/Spike
rip-off. don't do it, trilby!
```

Trilby was my username, and after that I stopped reading the comments. At least until I finished the book. And after that I was too scared. Too worried that I'd disappointed kc and darkangel and the other people who'd been following the story.

But after the break-up, as the summer started to end, I began again.

And you? You carried on too.

We all went to town one day: Georgie, Charlotte, JB and me. Finally time for me to buy that new notebook and start making a proper plan for the sequel. And it was nice to have Charlotte and Georgie hanging out again, the awkwardness between them finally starting to fade away now that it was clear Josh wasn't going anywhere. I could tell Charlotte still minded, just a bit, but she was trying, and I could tell that Georgie was grateful. Grateful enough that we all sat for hours, watching Charlotte try on dress after dress for the end-of-summer party at the Wheatsheaf.

'Come on, mate,' JB sighed, after she rejected the ninth or tenth. 'It's bloody roasting in here and you look great in everything you've tried on. Just pick one!'

Charlotte stuck her head back round the curtain. 'Um, you're supposed to enjoy this type of thing now, Jonathan – didn't anyone tell you?'

JB rolled his eyes. 'I'm gay, Char, not Gok Wan. Shopping is still boring and I'd much rather be in the pub. Can we go to the pub?'

'Just let me try on *one* more,' Charlotte said, ducking back into the cubicle.

'Why the big effort, babe?' Georgie asked, elbowing JB, who huffed and leaned back in his seat. 'I mean . . . it's only the Wheatsheaf, right?'

'Wouldn't have anything to do with Billy Butler from the year below, would it?' JB said, grinning slyly at me.

'No!' Charlotte's head popped out again, cheeks pink. 'Why, did he say something?'

JB laughed. 'I saw you guys talking at Azar's party the other night. He obviously fancies you.'

'I'm just making sure the new lower sixth feel welcome at the start of the year,' Charlotte said from behind the curtain, though we could all hear the smile in her voice.

'So, you gonna come to the party, Dais?' JB offered me his packet of gum. 'Last night of freedom and all that?'

'Oh, umm . . .' I hated the Wheatsheaf. It was OK in the day, but at night, with its sticky carpets and loud music and guys leering at girls, like us, who were too young to even be in there, it frightened me.

'Come on, you have to,' Georgie said, putting her arm round me. 'It'll be fun. We'll just sit in a corner and drink stupidly sweet drinks and watch everyone else make idiots of themselves.'

I glanced at JB. 'Will Logan be there?'

He chewed on his lip before answering. 'I'm not sure. I'm trying to persuade him but he's not keen to do much at the moment.'

'Don't worry about him,' Georgie said, not understanding. 'Look, it's our last night before everyone starts wanging on about A levels and uni again. Let's all go and get a bit drunk and a bit silly and have fun. It'll be good for you, Dais. It'll be good for all of us.'

I REMEMBER THAT evening, after Charlotte had finally chosen a dress and we'd all gone our separate ways home. My new notebook was sitting on the bed beside me, but even though the words had started to flow, I was still nervous about deciding exactly what was going to happen to Hannah in book two. Still scared of letting someone down, even with my silly story.

I flipped open my laptop and looked idly at the first book on StoryCity. I tried to remember how I'd felt writing that one, tried to get excited again about making something new. I read all of the comments users had left on each chapter, trying to soak them in. I sat and looked at the comments on the last chapter for the longest of all.

```
love this so much

aww man i was hoping Hannah would get
together with Lupa

this rocked so hard

soooo hope the basilisk shows up in the
sequel!
```

don't make us wait too long for the next
book, **trilby**!

Hannah Hass is my new idol. I wish I was
as badass as her

^^^ so agree with this. we all need to
be more like Hannah <3

I wanted to be more like Hannah then too.

And I still do. Even though Hannah's story is done now – I
finished it over Christmas just gone, a whole six months after
you all set off on that Malia holiday – I want to write again.
I want to tell my story, over and over.

I know you are afraid of that, Zack.

I DON'T REMEMBER that night, though of course you know that already.

Well, no, rewind – I remember the beginning at least. I remember getting ready round at Georgie's, Charlotte checking out her dress from every possible angle, JB cooking us all a couple of pizzas. We sat in the garden and drank wine his mum gave us while we ate.

'I thought eating was cheating,' Georgie said, nudging JB, but he just shrugged.

'Maybe the game isn't to get drunk as fast as possible any more. Maybe it's time we just started aiming to have a fun night?'

I chinked my glass against his and thought, *I can do that.*

I remember arriving too; David dropping us off, pushing a tenner at Georgie and JB so they could get a taxi home. I remember feeling happy in my outfit – a cute collared Sixties-style swing dress I found on eBay that swooshed around my thighs as I walked. I'd found laces the same colour yellow for my Converse and I felt like I'd stolen the last bit of summer and saved it up. I remember JB holding the door open for me, Charlotte's arm slinking through mine.

It was packed, wasn't it? Almost everyone from our year and the year below; loads of people from the year above, who were all getting ready to go to uni in a couple of weeks. It was some kind of charity night so the Wheatsheaf had booked a DJ and some lights and somehow the swoops of pink and red and green hid the sticky carpets and caught everyone's best side as they flashed by.

I looked around for people, for all of you. For Logan. JB had said he wasn't answering his phone that day and Nate hadn't spoken to him either. I'd thought about calling you, but something stopped me. I guess I was still angry with you for the way you'd treated JB. And, let's be honest, you and I have never been close. I always got the impression you thought I was boring. Not 'up for a laugh' enough. You said that once, when you thought I couldn't hear you. But I didn't really mind. I wasn't that bothered about being someone you thought was a laugh, which you probably noticed. So you kept your distance, mostly.

So it was a surprise, that night at the Wheatsheaf, when you came over to me.

But you did. You appeared on the other side of the bar and you headed right for us – for me. You gave me a hug, and you put a hand on my shoulder as you asked if I was OK. You'd heard about what happened, you said.

'How's Logan?' I asked, and your face creased. With concern maybe, or confusion.

'He's fine,' you said, and even though I wanted that to be a good thing, the words sliced into me. Just a little.

You asked if you could buy me a drink, and I said yes. I needed it suddenly. I was thinking that perhaps I was wrong;

238

perhaps Logan had just wanted to break up and that was it. There was nothing secretly wrong or anything he was hiding. He just didn't want to be with me.

You bought me a glass of wine and you stood beside me while I sipped it.

'Not really your scene, is it?' you said, but you didn't make it sound like a bad thing.

'Can't hurt to have a change,' I said, and I took another big sip of wine. I wanted to ask you if Logan was coming but I wasn't sure what I needed the answer to be.

'That's what I always say,' you said, and you winked at me.

Charlotte came back from the toilet and you disappeared into the crowd again. I drank the drink you'd bought me and then I bought myself another. I hadn't eaten much of the pizza and my head felt lighter, it felt quieter. I sang along to the songs the DJ was playing as they turned down the lights, and when Charlotte suggested a bottle of wine, so we wouldn't have to keep going to the bar, I agreed.

People say now – I hear them, I'm sure you do too – that it wasn't enough to be as drunk as I say I was. Girls at school spent weeks listing all of the times they've drunk a couple of vodkas and a few glasses of wine and been fine. They say I'm a liar because somehow that's easier to believe than the idea that I am a lightweight. But I am. I always have been.

We spoke again later – just like you told everyone. I was at a table near the edge of the dance floor, pouring the last of the bottle into my glass while Charlotte talked to Billy Butler, who'd been eyeing her up all night. You came up, asked me if I was having a good time.

I smiled and I told you I was.

I should tell you now that I've thought about that conversation a lot. I wonder what I said or what you saw that made you think the way you did.

But I don't remember. I just don't.

I remember dancing. We all do. Me and Charlotte and Nate and Dev; Hope too. Faces smiling back at me, the crappy disco lights shading them pink and then green and then blue. Another bottle of wine was bought, but then Charlotte loomed over me, a glass of water in her hand. I pushed her away; I pulled her close and kissed her cheek.

I fell. Aiming for a chair or perhaps just losing which way was up, my weight spilling back onto the floor. Dev was there, helping me up. *You OK, Dais? Want some water?*

And then you. Arm steering me away from the dance floor, to a bench outside. *I've got her, guys. She's all right.*

I REMEMBER THAT morning, the way my eyelids stuck together as I tried to open them, the inside of my mouth thick and dry. There was a pain in my head which worsened every time I moved – just a hangover headache, I thought, but when I put my hand to the back of my head I felt a bump there.

When I sat up, things started coming back to me – small snatches of time, fluttering through my head without settling. JB helping me out of a taxi, my mum helping me into bed. I cringed, wishing I could throw the duvet back over myself.

There was something else too – a memory of opening my eyes and looking up at a patch of starry sky, the ground hard underneath me. I ran my hands over the backs of my legs and found small, painful lumps there. Pieces of gravel. I pulled them out as I tried to stop the pounding behind my eyes.

And then you. I remembered you. Leading me out of the pub, laughing. I remembered your voice, raised, JB's even louder.

But the words wouldn't come. The words were gone.

I got in the shower and got ready for school.

I was late to registration after enduring my mum's lecture about drinking too much, drinking on a school night, embarrassing myself and my friends. I let her work her way onto how polite

241

and nice JB was, her anger running out of steam, and then made for the door with a piece of toast I couldn't really stomach.

It's just Charlotte and me in my form – no you, no Logan, no JB or Georgie or Nate or Dev. For some reason I didn't understand, I felt relieved about that as I hurried in and took my seat next to her.

Miss Elsworth glanced up as she marked me in, but the rest of the room was lost in conversation, people catching up after the summer. Charlotte gave me an odd look.

'You OK?'

I nodded. 'Feel quite rough.'

'What happened to you last night? You just disappeared. I thought we were getting a taxi home together.'

I felt my face turn hot. 'I was so drunk, I don't know . . . JB took me home, I think.'

'You think?'

'No, he did. I'm sorry, Char. Did you have a good night though?'

But she didn't answer me. She was fiddling with the ring on her thumb and then she looked up at me.

'Dais . . . did something happen with you and Zack?'

My stomach lurched. Your name had been there that whole time, lodged in my head, my throat. I just hadn't wanted to hear it, to bring it out and think about how it got there.

'No!' My face was getting hotter, sweat cooling on my back. 'Of course not. Who said that?'

'A lot of people. Apparently you guys went to the car park to have *sex*.' She whispered the last part. 'That's not true, surely.'

'Of course it's not,' I said, but there was a sour taste in my

242

mouth, the memory of that patch of sky again. When the bell went for first period, I had to stop myself from running for the door.

It was Dev I saw first. He caught up to me halfway across the playground, those neon Wayfarers tucked into the neck of his polo shirt. 'All right, Dais?'

'Hi.' I kept my head down, feeling eyes on my skin as people passed me.

'Good night last night?'

'Mmm.' Watching loose crumbs of asphalt skidding under people's feet reminded me of the balls of granite I'd picked out of my skin that morning. The bump on the back of my head pulsed.

'Look, I think it's cool,' Dev said, slinging an arm round my shoulders. 'You and Zack. Don't think Lo's gonna like it, but I'll back you guys up.'

I shrugged him off. My skin felt white-hot and I couldn't bear his touch. 'Me and Zack are not a thing, Dev. How could you think that?'

His face creased in confusion. 'But last night . . .'

Last night last night last night. It thudded through me but all that echoed back was emptiness: *I can't remember*.

'What happened last night?' I asked, forcing myself to look Dev in the eye.

He was still looking confused. 'You and Zack . . . you guys left the party together. You were all over each other–'

'Daisy.' JB jogged up beside me. 'You OK? I need to talk to you.'

'I'll leave you guys to it,' Dev said, walking backwards with

243

his palms held up. 'Catch you later.' And he turned and walked back towards Main Block – and with a sense of dread, I saw you appear there, lost in conversation with a guy from your form. A shark swimming towards me as I waited in my cage.

And then JB's hand closed around mine, and he pulled me into the art block, out of sight.

'Daisy, are you OK?' he asked again, and then: 'Daisy, do you remember?'

And I shook my head and didn't know which question I was answering. 'Did I –' I shook my head again, the words too wrong to even come out. 'People are saying I slept with Zack.'

JB's lips turned thin, his eyes fixed on mine. 'You didn't.'

I nodded then, relief flooding through me.

'You were out of it, Dais . . .'

I remembered stumbling on the dance floor, laughing faces yawning over me, a forest of hands stretching out to pick me up. 'I fell over.'

'Yeah, you did. Look, I don't know how to explain this . . . Zack . . . Zack and you were dancing a bit and then you kept falling over. And he said he was taking you outside for some air.'

It didn't sound like you. But the story kept coming.

HERE'S HOW IT goes:

    You say you kissed me.

    You say I kissed you back.

    I say I cannot remember.

    You say you asked me if I wanted to go somewhere.

    You say I said yes.

    I say I cannot remember.

    I say I can't imagine saying that.

You say you led me away from the pub, to somewhere more private. The place you chose was the empty staff car park behind the supermarket.

    You say that on the way there I fell over. Twice. You say I laughed.

    The scrapes and cuts on my shins and my elbows agree with you.

    You say that we kissed against a wall, a wall that helped keep me upright.

    You say that when we fell, we fell together.

    We lay there together.

    We were in it together.

Nate and JB say they came out to find me and saw you on top
of me on the ground.

They say that my skirt was pushed all the way up.

They say that I wasn't moving.

When they pulled you off, you said they didn't understand.

You said we were just having some fun.

I say I cannot remember.

'I DON'T UNDERSTAND.' My pulse thudding again, wine still churning in my belly. 'You're saying he –'

I didn't understand what he was saying you did or wanted to do or could have done.

JB was leaning against a wall. He looked down at the floor and did not look at me.

'I'm saying that you were passed out, and he was on top of you. Nate and me, we pulled him off you before . . . before anything happened.'

'You're saying . . .'

I didn't finish that sentence. We looked at each other.

'Daisy, whatever you want to do, I'll back you,' JB said.

I moved away, straightened the strap of my bag across my body. 'What is there to do?'

'I mean, if you wanted to report him . . .'

'No.' I surprised myself; perhaps now I'm surprising you too. 'Nothing happened. It's nothing.'

It was nothing and yet it was everything, wasn't it? In other people's heads, in other people's mouths, you and I had so many stories.

We were getting together, we were a one-night stand. It was

247

the first time, it wasn't. I chased you, you'd always wanted me. I was on a rebound, I'd dumped Logan for you.

Logan.

I thought of him first; did you? How he'd feel when he heard that rumour, what he'd think of me. I kept picking up my phone to text him, but couldn't find the words. Because I couldn't remember.

And then it was lunchtime and Charlotte linked her arm through mine and walked me to the common room. 'Just ignore them,' she said. But I hadn't told her what JB had said – those words were lost as well and I was too scared to even try to look for them.

But other words rang out clear. Joni Hart whispered, 'Slag,' as I passed; 'What a bitch,' muttered Ben Williams to his friends. By the time you appeared, Charlotte and I were tucked in a corner and I didn't hear the words everyone had for you.

And then there was Logan. There was you, Zack, laughing about something with Marcus, and not even noticing Logan shoving his way past the boys milling around you. Not even noticing him until his toes were touching yours and his fists were full of your shirt, pulling you close to him.

And everyone heard the words you said then.

'Don't cry about it, Logan. Just because she fancied a go with a real man.'

The room got quiet then, even quieter, until all I could hear was Logan breathing, his knuckles turning pale as he gripped you. Nate thundering into the room just a few steps behind, trying to get through the crowd that was gathering. And behind you that big plate-glass window and everyone waiting to see who would end up thrown through it.

But Logan didn't push you. You'll remember that.

He put his face close to yours and he said: *Call yourself a man.*

And then he let you go and he walked away.

Though he didn't look at me as he passed.

I HID IN my room that night, watching *Game of Thrones* on the projector with my laptop lid flipped low so I couldn't see any of the messages that popped up. Charlotte, Georgie, JB. Joni Hart asking why I'd been such a bitch to Logan. Your friend Marcus asking if I wanted to come for drinks with 'the boys' at the weekend.

There was a knock at the door. I didn't want to answer. I wasn't very good at pretending to my parents that I was all right when I wasn't, but I tried to put on my best 'OK' face and paused the film. 'Come in'.

Except it wasn't my parents. It was Hope Novak.

She stood in the doorway, dressed in leggings and a hoodie, her light hair in a ponytail. 'Hi,' she said.

'Hi.'

She came over and sat on the end of the bed. I sat up properly and we faced each other, cross-legged.

'Nate told me what happened,' she said. 'You doing OK?'

I shrugged, as if that might stop her words from sticking around long enough for me to think about them. 'I don't remember what happened,' I said. I wanted that to be the end of the discussion, but Hope seemed to think I was protecting you.

'Nate does,' she said. 'You know he was driving, right? He was completely sober.'

I picked up my Marauder's Map cushion and hugged it to my chest.

'Look,' Hope said, 'I get that you probably don't want to talk about this. But I just wanted to check you were all right.'

My fingers found a thick patch of stitching – Hogsmeade, I thought, tracing the roofs – and I nodded. 'I'm fine. I just . . .'

I trailed off and Hope let me. We both watched the paused image on the projector screen: Jon Snow looking pensive, one hand on the hilt of his sword, while a blizzard swirled behind him.

'I heard about Logan starting on him today,' Hope said, reaching up to pull her ponytail tighter. 'You know Logan knows you wouldn't do it, right?'

I realised I was chewing my bottom lip and pressed the top one against it to stop myself. My fingers found the turrets of Hogwarts and I tried to focus on tracing them.

'It's nice of you to come,' I said eventually. 'I'm all right though.'

My laptop bleeped again, followed by the buzz of my phone. It was close to Hope's foot and I glanced down at it a second after she did; saw the preview on the lock screen too late to pull it away. Marcus.

```
Don't be like that. I know you like a
good time ;)
```

I kept on looking at it even as the screen turned dark again. I could feel Hope's eyes on me.

'Marcus is a prick,' she said.

'I don't care about him.'

'Nate and JB won't let people talk about you like that,' Hope said. 'Neither will I.'

I shrugged. 'I drank too much. I don't even remember.'

'Whoa.' Hope leaned back against the bed frame. 'Daisy, don't do that. It doesn't matter *how* much you had to drink. It doesn't matter how much *he* had to drink. Nate and JB had to pull him off your unconscious body.'

I stared at her. She was the first to look away.

'I'm sorry,' she said eventually. 'I didn't come here to have a go at you. I just . . . I wanted to let you know that I'm here. If you need me.' She glanced back up at me. 'Is that weird?'

I shook my head. 'No. Thank you.'

She glanced up at the screen again. 'I love this episode. Do you want to watch the rest?'

And that's how I ended up sitting on my bed with my ex-boyfriend's ex-girlfriend, watching TV and saying nothing.

HERE'S WHAT USUALLY happens:

A rumour starts.

A rumour spreads.

People whisper and giggle and get bored.

The rumour fades and another takes over.

But people didn't get bored of this one, did they? People loved the idea of quiet, boring Daisy shagging her ex-boyfriend's best mate up against a supermarket wall. Especially the way you told it.

They didn't like Hope's version of the story quite so much.

We spent a lot of time together that week, Hope and I. Georgie and Charlotte. At lunch we went into town and tucked ourselves into a corner of the cafe where no one else goes; after school we hung out in bedrooms and watched box sets and ate whole cakes. And Hope or Char or Georgie would try to tell me how someone else had been talking about you and me, and how they had set them straight. I would cut myself another piece of cake, or find the remote, and wait until the conversation moved on. I guess I was still hoping it would all go away; that someone else would do something new.

But of course, that someone was you.

It was just Hope and me in the corner of the common room that break-time – Charlotte had a free period and had gone for a driving lesson, and Georgie was off sick. Hope was showing me a video on her phone of a dog that could supposedly say 'bacon', and we were sharing a bag of strawberry laces. We didn't notice you until you were standing in front of us, your arms folded.

It was the first time I'd seen you properly since the party. Three days of keeping my head down on my way to lessons, of ducking out to the cafe and to the park when I had nowhere to be. And then you were just standing there, collar turned up, a paper coffee cup from the place down town in your hand.

'I need to talk to you,' you said, and your eyes moved from Hope to me.

'Fuck off, Zack,' Hope said, but your gaze stayed on me. I looked away and I tried not to think of the bump on the back of my head, of JB's face as he pulled me into the art block corridor that Monday morning.

'Daisy,' you said, as if you couldn't believe I'd dared to look away. 'You've gotta stop this.'

'Zack,' Hope said, straightening in her seat. 'I'm warning you –'

'It's OK,' I said, interrupting her. I stood up. Do you remember that? 'Stop what exactly, Zack?'

People were looking, of course they were. People are always looking, aren't they?

But you didn't like it. You took a step closer, you lowered your voice. 'Stop saying you didn't want it,' you hissed. 'Stop getting your *minions* –' you glared at Hope – 'to tell people I . . . *forced* myself on you just cos you feel guilty.'

'I'm not getting *anyone* to do *anything*,' I said, and my voice sounded calmer than I'd expected, though I could barely hear it over the blood pulsing in my ears. 'Nate and JB are just telling people what they saw.'

You flinched – but just a little. And then you laughed.

'Daisy, come on. Everyone else is just saying what *they* saw. You were *all* over me, it was kind of pathetic. You spent half the night talking to me, laughing at my jokes and getting me to buy you drinks. You were desperate for me to make a move.'

I was quiet then; you took that as a victory, I think. You looked around, trying to build on it. You didn't seem to understand that your words had taken my breath away.

'Isn't that right, Dev?' you asked. I hadn't even noticed him behind you, his phone in one hand, a bottle of Lucozade in the other. He came towards you, looking awkward.

'Isn't what right?'

'Daisy,' you said, and you were looking at him then. 'Daisy was all over me last weekend, wasn't she? She was giving me the come-on big time.'

Dev wasn't looking at me then either. He glanced at Hope. 'Well . . . yeah.' People were crowding around now, eager to hear the fight. You and I were hot gossip again. You looked at Dev and he nodded, tapping the Lucozade bottle against his leg. 'You did seem pretty keen, Dais.'

'It's difficult to be keen when you're unconscious,' Hope said, standing up too. 'Come on, Daisy. You don't have to listen to this.'

You stared at me and I tried not to look away.

'You wanted it,' you said, and though the words wouldn't come, I still managed to shake my head.

THAT EVENING, HOPE took me to play squash. I hadn't played for ages, not since my parents signed me up for lessons as a kid, but Hope's dad was a semi-pro when he was younger and he lent us a couple of his rackets and dropped us at the courts. It felt good, hammering the ball around, Hope breathing hard beside me. When our arms were aching and both of us had round bruises on our bare legs from the ball, we walked out into the warm evening and went to mine.

We took it in turns to shower and then we sat on my bed in our pyjamas, *Goblet of Fire* on the screen and a bottle of wine Hope had brought with her to keep us company. It hit me that there were two whole days of weekend ahead of us, no school – but then my phone buzzed with a message.

```
You out tonight? ;)
```

Some guy from the year above who I'd never even spoken to. I hit the off button. I hadn't posted a new chapter all week either and I was starting to get comments about it on the previous one, people wondering when something new would be uploaded.

'You OK?' Hope asked, leaning over to top up my wine.

'Yeah.' I turned to her. 'Hey, thanks for today.'

She took a big gulp of her wine. 'No problem. I still say you should tell someone about what happened.'

'I can't. I don't even remember really – and *nothing* actually happened.'

'But only because –'

'We don't know that, Hope. We don't know what would've happened.'

She sighed. 'Are you gonna open that Haribo or what?'

I reached at random for one of the four bags we'd bought on the way home. I opened it and took a handful before passing it over. We sat and watched Harry run his bath as my mouth filled with Haribo egg foam.

'Look, Daisy, I feel like you've been open with me about all this stuff. Maybe I owe you some of that in return.'

I turned on my side to look at her. 'What do you mean?'

'This . . . whole thing has made me think. A lot. And I'm not trying to say I know how you feel. At all. But.' She stopped and we were both quiet as Moaning Myrtle put the moves on Harry. 'I guess . . . well, this *thing* happened when we were on holiday.'

I was surprised, later, that my first thought wasn't Logan. But it didn't cross my mind. I knew they wouldn't do that to me.

Instead I just said: 'OK.'

'It was the night before the last one, and we went on this big booze cruise to some island and it all got . . . out of hand.'

'That was the night on that TV show?'

Hope winced. 'Yeah, I think so. I didn't really watch it.'

Harry was under the water, listening to the mermaids sing.

'I was out of it,' Hope said quietly. 'I can't even remember the end of the night. I . . . I woke up on the beach the next morning, no idea how I got there.' She picked up a cola bottle but didn't eat it. 'My dress was pulled up, everyone could see. These two Scouse boys woke me up and tried to help me get home.'

'Where were the others?'

She shrugged. 'They were all wasted. They went home.'

'They didn't even notice you were gone?'

'I guess not.' She dropped the cola bottle and picked up a jelly ring, sliding it down her finger until it rested on the first knuckle. 'It was a really messed-up night.'

'Do you think . . .' My mouth felt dry. 'Hope, are you saying something happened to you?'

She shook her head. 'No. I don't think so. I didn't . . . I didn't feel any different, if you know what I mean.' She glanced at me. 'Look, Daisy, I've driven myself crazy trying to remember stuff from that night, imagining what could've happened, but I can't. I can't remember, and I hate that. I know you're probably doing the same. But that's my whole point. I don't want you to beat yourself up for accidentally having a drink or three too many. It happens.' She flicked the jelly ring off and stared at it. 'It's *not* an invitation. To anyone.'

I swallowed hard. 'I know that.'

We sat and watched Harry and Hermione trying to figure out the second riddle.

'They should have looked after you,' I said quietly.

'Yeah, they should. But I feel like all of them have completely forgotten what being a friend is supposed to mean, to be honest.

Like, how many times have you heard Dev say, "Bros before hoes"? But then the day Nate's sister died, where was Dev?'

I shrugged and shook my head. I didn't even know Nate or Dev then, not really.

'He was round Mollie's, trying to persuade her to sleep with him, as per.'

'Oh.'

'And then there's Logan,' Hope continued, her voice getting louder, not seeming to notice the painful ache hearing his name gave me. 'Anyone who spends more than ten minutes with him can tell he's having a hard time. But will he tell any of them about it? Will they ask him?'

'No,' I said, but the faint shrill of the doorbell had distracted me.

'Like, to quote our good friend Mr Weasley, they *need* to sort out their priorities.'

'Hope,' I said.

'Yeah, I know, I'm getting worked up, but it's just –'

'*Hope.*'

She stopped talking and looked at me.

'There's someone downstairs,' I said.

We crept to the edge of the landing, though the voices were already carrying up: the murmured protests of my dad. The rumbling demands of yours.

'– need to keep that daughter of yours under control,' he was saying, as Hope pressed close to me against the banister. 'She can't go round making claims like that. Could ruin a boy's future, a rumour like that.'

259

'I'm not sure I understand what you mean,' my dad said, and a thrill of fear went through me. My quiet, kind dad. Me and you, slumped against a supermarket wall.

'Your daughter, going round that school accusing my boy of rape.' Your dad is loud. The word reverberated around our narrow hall, bouncing up, up, up to Hope and me. 'I won't have it. You don't get to slag yourself around a party, leading lads on, and then cry rape when someone takes you up on it. You need to tell her that. You need to control your daughter.'

'My daughter is a good girl.' My dad is small and I'm sure he was intimidated. I could hear my mum coming in from the study, trying to interrupt, see what was wrong. But my dad stayed calm. 'I don't know what you're talking about, but Daisy does not lie. I would like you to leave now.'

I could only imagine what was going through his head then. Imagining me. Lying. Raped. *Slagging myself around*.

'She was drunk and threw herself at him,' your dad said. The words sounded wet; spit landing on my dad's skin. 'I've got the whole story, mate. Doesn't sound like you have. But I'm telling you –' The thud of his boots on the hall floor, steps taken closer, the shadow of his jabbing finger stretching up the wall with every word. 'My boy doesn't deserve to have his whole life ruined for ten minutes of action, just because *your daughter* felt bad about her boyfriend after they were done. And I'll make sure that doesn't happen. Just so you know. I'll make sure of it.'

'Stay here. I'm not listening to this,' Hope said, and before I realised I could move, release my white-knuckled fingers from their grip on the banister, she was gone, fluffy socks flashing past me.

'Girls like yours –' Gordon was saying. 'Oh, hello, Hope.'

'What are you doing here?' Hope's voice, firm, loud. Finally bubbling up and covering the words he'd let loose in my house.

And me, sitting there. Doing nothing.

'Hope, I get that Daisy is your friend. But so's Zack –'

'Zack's not my friend. And Daisy is not a liar.'

'Well, you would say that, she's your mate – and I respect that, Hope, I do. But boys will be boys and your little friend needs to learn that. You can't just strut around a party being a total prick-tease –'

'Please,' my dad said. 'Please leave now. We're calling the police.'

'If they call the police, Gordon,' Hope said, 'I'll tell them that everything Daisy says is true. I'll tell them how Zack joked about me being easy and a slag when we were on holiday, and I'll tell them how a girl he fancied when we were away went missing the day before we left.'

Your dad was silent; I could hear his mouth gape. And still I didn't move.

'There's no need for talk like that,' he said, and I heard our door handle turn. 'But let's just put this to bed, eh? So to speak.' And as the outside air rushed in, I heard him laugh at his choice of words.

'They weren't in bed, Gordon,' Hope said. 'She was passed out in a car park and your son was on top of her.'

And she closed the door on him.

IT TOOK SOME time to calm my parents down. It took me, standing in between them, trying to explain. Hope sitting at our kitchen counter, trying to back me up. My mum, her business head on, trying to reason things out, explain how we could make it better. My dad, family man, afraid and out of his depth. But eventually they let us go.

Eventually I could ask what Hope had meant about the girl you met on holiday.

'She was lovely,' she said, not sitting down. Standing. Her shoulders and palms resting against my wall, eyes focused on her feet. She was too wired, she said. Couldn't sit. 'Emily. She's still missing, you know. Her mate messaged me.'

'What, and you think Zack had something to do with it?' I couldn't bring myself to think it. I wonder if that makes you feel better.

Hope thought about it for a while. She thought about it for a long, long time, until the *Goblet* credits were running on the screen behind her.

'No,' she said. 'I'm not calling Zack a murderer.' Her face crumpled. 'Not that I'm saying she –'

'She could be OK,' I said, quickly trying to fill the gap.

'Yeah, she could. I hope so.'

We were silent for a minute. 'That's so awful,' I said, and Hope nodded.

'Ness said the police found CCTV footage of her getting in a car with some guy who worked at one of the bars. The theory is that they ran away together, but Ness says Emily would never have done that.' She reached for my laptop and flipped it open, typing into the search bar. 'Here,' she said. 'This is her.'

My eyes flicked over the article, my heart sinking.

British police have today combed a stretch of beach in Malia where Sussex-born tourist Emily Simpson was last seen [. . .]

Emily, a well-known party girl, had enjoyed all of Malia's attractions – including a booze-soaked boat party – during her week-long holiday, and witnesses said that she'd been seeing getting close to several fellow revellers over the days prior to her disappearance [. . .]

CCTV footage showed Emily getting into a car looking very pleased with her companion for the evening, later identified as bar manager Thomas Kingsford [. . .]

Emily texted pals: 'Am safe. Love you.'

[. . .] The whereabouts of Thomas Kingsford are currently unknown.

I stared at the picture on the article, uniformed police huddled on an empty beach, a sun-lounger left abandoned on the sand. I tried not to let the words pierce me, but one by one they wormed their way in. *party girl . . . enjoyed . . . booze . . .*

'They're blaming her,' I said.

'I know.'

After Hope left, I looked through the search results again, thinking of missing Emily Simpson. Did her parents think it was her daughter's fault for getting into a car with a stranger?

Do you remember when that girl from Abbots Grey went missing and people said how stupid she was for talking to strangers online?

Everyone was saying it was my fault, what happened or didn't happen that night at the Wheatsheaf. Your friends and your dad were saying it for you, the words flooding my social media feeds – needling words that didn't mention my name but were meant for me anyway. *innocent until proven guilty. It's a shame sum1 has to tell lies cos they regrettin being a slut.* All that weekend, the boys from your rugby team filled my inboxes, telling me that they *saw* me, that I was *all over* you that night. They called me heartless. They called me a slag. They called me a lying little girl.

I wanted to reply.

Instead, I lost myself in Hannah's story again.

WHEN MONDAY MORNING arrived, I was up and showered early, even though I was willing the hours to stretch and last before I had to go to school. I was restless, hadn't slept well. I'd spent the whole weekend writing chapter after chapter, empty food packets and tea mugs building up in a tide around my bed. But as soon as Sunday evening rolled around, I couldn't concentrate. A cool feeling of dread building, even though I wouldn't let myself admit it or examine it. And then a night full of weird, half-formed dreams until I'd given up just after 5 a.m. and switched on the light to read.

There were still forty minutes until Charlotte, who'd passed her driving test on Friday, was going to pick me up, so I opened my laptop and sat back down on the bed with it. I pulled up the homepage of StoryCity and clicked into my notifications.

I was pleased with the work I'd done over the weekend. I'd lost myself in it, in being Hannah, thinking like Hannah, and somehow the story had flowed. A haunted house, a family troubled by what Hannah suspected was a poltergeist though I wasn't sure how the story would pan out just yet. It had felt good though, describing plates smashing, doors slamming, furniture hurled to the ground. And being back with Hannah had felt good too. As her, I'd argued with Tobias and gone to a bar, trying to get inside information on the family who claimed to be haunted. I invented a new problem for her to handle – a film being made of one of her most famous novels, and the media asking awkward questions about the inspiration behind it. I stalked through streets with her and I worried about her worries and fought her fights and the weekend had disappeared, just like that.

And people seemed to like it too, which was a relief. There were nice comments, including one from kcinthecity:

```
yaaaaaaaay! welcome back trilby! SO
EXCITED ABOUT THIS!
```

I wished I could just stay in my room for another couple of days, carry on writing. I wanted to spend my time there, with those friends, with kc and darkangel and all the others, reading their work and losing myself in their worlds too.

But then my eyes kept straying to the other open tabs at the top of my browser – all articles about Emily Simpson. I couldn't stop myself from reading and rereading those articles, and the comments left beneath them by people who thought Emily Simpson had brought whatever happened to her on herself by going out, by drinking, by flirting.

I closed my laptop lid and got up to pack my bag.

I figured maybe it'd be good for me to get out of the house.

THE DAY PASSED quickly, my busiest of the week with double maths in the morning and then biology and history in the afternoon. I spent the free in the middle trying to catch up on the biology homework I'd forgotten about, and trying not to google Emily Simpson.

Char had a free at the end of the day, and so did Georgie and JB. They'd messaged, asking if I wanted them to wait for me, but it'd been a quiet day and I was feeling OK about things. It was warm outside and I told them I didn't mind walking.

I checked my phone. A message from Charlotte.

Call me later if u want to hang out ☺

I hadn't seen Hope since Friday night. We didn't have any lessons together, and I'd stayed in the library for lunch, finishing the last biology questions with my headphones in. I hadn't seen anyone, really, apart from Char in the morning and JB in biology. Maybe that was why things felt quiet.

I was the last to pack up my things and leave the classroom, kids streaming out of the main school and flooding across the playground. I stuck my earbuds in and slid my sunglasses on, the wind skittering through the trees and sending dappled yellow light across the concrete. I walked slowly out of the gates, letting the crowds disappear ahead of me, turning my music up loud and letting my mind wander.

'Hey!' A hand on my shoulder made my heart jump into my throat. I yanked my earphones out and spun round.

'Hi.'

Nate.

'Sorry, I didn't mean to scare you. Was calling but, you know . . .' He gestured to his ears.

'Yeah. Was a Beatles sort of a day.'

'You heading home?'

'Yep.'

'Mind if I walk with you for a bit?'

I clicked my music off and stuck my earphones into my satchel. 'Sure, why not.'

We set off down the hill, my bag bumping against my thigh, Nate's hands in his pockets.

'So, Daisy, I know we haven't spoken since the other night . . .'

I glanced behind me, a painful jolt in my chest. *I don't want to talk about that.*

'It's OK,' I said, trying to stop him finishing his thought. 'JB . . . JB told me. Thank you. For, you know. What you guys did.'

Nate glanced sideways at me. 'I overheard some of the rugby team at lunch. Have people been sending you messages?'

I shifted the strap of my bag, pushed my sunglasses back up my nose. 'It's nothing. Honestly. It's fine.'

'No, it isn't. That's what I wanted to say to you. It's not OK, and I won't let it happen. Neither will Hope or JB, or your mates.'

I swallowed hard, glad that my eyes were hidden behind my sunglasses. 'Thanks. It'll all blow over, it's fine.'

'Just so long as you know we're here.'

We hit the main road and waited for a gap in the traffic. And even though I'd meant to keep them in, the words drifted out.

'How's Logan?'

Nate took a deep breath in, ran a hand over his short hair. He looked down at me. 'I don't think he's doing great, Dais.'

My voice came out smaller than I'd expected. 'No.'

'I'm trying, you know.' Nate put a palm on my back, prompting me across the road. We had to jog to make it before a van rushed past. 'Just have to keep checking in on him, trying to get him out, that kinda thing. But he's in a bit of a dark place, I think.'

'Can I do anything?'

He shrugged. 'I think we just all need to be there for him.'

'Kind of hard when he won't talk to me.' And it was true – at least partly. I'd sent a couple of messages before school started, had even tried calling the night of the party at the Wheatsheaf when we first got there and the wine was first filling me with warmth. He hadn't replied. But I hadn't tried to get in touch with him since then either.

Nate put an arm round me. 'I'm gonna keep talking to him, don't worry.'

'I'll keep trying too,' I said, and suddenly I meant it.

I LAY IN bed that night with my phone held up above my face, trying to compose a message to Logan. There were so many things I wanted to say; how I was worried about him, how I wanted us to be friends, to look after each other. But the truth was, I was still hurt by the way things had ended between us. By the way he had faced up to you, dismissing you and what you said – but still ignoring me. I wanted to be bigger than that, to reach out to him when he obviously needed a friend. But it hurt.

In the end I settled for easy, for bland: *Hope you're* OK.

And then later, awake again, I gave in and typed the thing I really wanted to say.

I miss you.

The next day, I woke to a text from JB.

```
Hey Dais. It's my birthday today so
a bunch of us are going to go to the
meadow for lunch. Wanna come? x
```

I sat up and smiled, typed back quickly.

> Happy birthday lovely! And yeah! What
> shall I bring? x

I walked to school that morning too, stopping at the deli to buy a couple of cheeses, some of the good bread (and yes, of course I felt a pang then, remembering afternoons spent in the park with Logan – but my phone stayed silent, no buzz of a message from him) and a box of *really* good brownies. I'd paid and packed it all into a canvas tote and was getting ready to leave, when I heard a familiar voice in one of the aisles.

'They don't have it, Mum. I told you they don't!'

I moved carefully in its direction, my heart thudding.

'Yeah, yeah, OK. I'll go to the health-food place after school. No, I don't mind.'

I peeked around a shelf of olives, the tote on my shoulder catching one of the jars. I reached out to grab it before it could fall, and when I turned back, there he was. Looking back at me.

'Hey, Dais.'

'Hi, Dev.'

He nodded at the phone in his hand. 'My mum sent me to look for some random kind of pasta. What you doing here?'

'It's JB's birthday.' I touched the bag on my shoulder. 'We're going to the meadow for lunch. Cheese, beer, that kind of thing.'

He nodded. 'Ah yeah, forgot it was today. I should text him.'

I stared at him. 'You should come for lunch.'

'Yeah . . .' He glanced down at his feet. 'Maybe.'

I felt hot suddenly, the words boiling over. 'What's the problem, Dev? Me or JB?'

271

'What?' His eyes wide, hands held up to hide the lie. 'There's no problem, Dais. I haven't got a problem with anyone.'

'Yeah, right.' I turned on my heel and left the shop, trying to calm my heart.

But Dev followed me. He caught up to me halfway down the road, outside the little crappy hairdressers my parents used to take me to when I was a kid.

'Daisy, I know things are a bit weird at the moment but –'

'You took his side,' I said. I kept walking.

'Zack's my friend,' he said. 'I'm just trying to stick by him –'

'By calling me a liar. Me, Nate, JB.'

'Daisy, nothing *actually* happened –'

I stopped then; turned to face him, the bag of food dropped and forgotten at my feet. 'Do you ever think for yourself, Dev? Instead of just parroting whatever Zack tells you to?'

His hands were up again, his face bewildered like my words were silly, girly slaps he needed to fend off. 'I dunno what you mean, Dais . . .'

'Yes, you do. Agreeing with him that I was all over him that night when I know, I *know*, that you don't believe that, Dev. Ignoring JB just because Zack feels uncomfortable about him being gay. And I bet you're ignoring Logan now too, aren't you? All because of Zack.'

A funny thing happened then, Zack. Because Dev didn't defend you. He didn't try to explain it all away.

He started to cry.

'Shit,' he said, turning away from me. 'Shit.' He pushed the tears away before they'd even really begun, and then he sat down on the edge of the kerb. And I sat down next to him.

272

'It's all a mess, Dais,' he said, taking his Wayfarers from the neck of his T-shirt and pushing them onto his face. 'The whole group's fallen apart.'

'It hasn't. But you're acting like you've chosen your side. How can you treat JB like that, Dev? You guys have been friends for so long.'

'I know.' He propped his head on his hand, turned his face to look at me. 'I feel bad. I do feel bad.' His voice wobbled, and he turned to look at the road again. 'But Zack . . . Zack's my man, you know? He's always looked out for me.'

'Has he?'

'Yeah, course. Like the time me and Mollie had a fight at that party in London and she went and stayed at her cousin's without me. Zack paid for me to get a taxi all the way back here and stay at his.'

I kept quiet. It was a nice thing you did, sure. But did it mean anything, really, to you?

'You don't get it, Daisy. You don't know what it's like.'

'What what's like?'

'I'm . . . I'm not anything. Dhruv is the smart one, the one my parents are proud of. And then in the group, it's the same. Nate's the good-looking one, the one who gets all the girls. Zack and Logan are good at sports. JB's the popular one, the funny one. I'm not . . . I'm not anything special. Do you know how lucky I am that Zack wants to hang around with me?'

'Do you know how lucky *he* is that you do?' I reached out and put a hand over his. 'Seriously, Dev, is that really what you think of yourself?'

He shrugged. 'I had a good thing with Mollie, and I messed

273

that up. I had a good thing with my mates, and I've messed that up too. My results are average, and I don't really know what I'll end up doing after this year – not like you, or Char, or JB, or Zack.' He glanced at me. 'I'm not trying to throw myself a pity party or anything, Dais. I'm just trying to explain to you. Zack's been good to me; he always makes sure I'm included in stuff, part of things. You know? I know he's not perfect, but he's my mate. I'm not gonna just turn on him.'

'But you must see that it's not OK how he's treating JB?'

Dev bit his bottom lip. 'He'll get over it . . . I know he will.'

I withdrew my hand, picked up my bag. 'Maybe,' I said, standing up. 'But maybe, in the meantime, you need to do something more than just standing by and hoping things will all work out.'

DEV DIDN'T MAKE it to the picnic at lunch; we didn't see either of you in the common room that day. JB said Logan had texted to say happy birthday, but there was no sign of him at school either.

But the rest of us walked down to the meadow together, stopping to pick up cans of drink and bags of sweets and crisps from the newsagents in town on the way. It was still stupidly warm, lazy like a summer Saturday instead of a Tuesday halfway through September. We climbed over the stile and walked through the long grass, JB, Hope and Nate up ahead; me, Charlotte and Georgie behind. Georgie was telling us about a party Josh had mentioned that was happening that weekend, Charlotte wondering aloud if Billy might be there.

We found a spot in the shorter grass and Hope spread out the blanket she'd brought with her. I'd brought one too, and Georgie had a big scarf she'd found in her locker. I laid out the food I'd picked up from the deli, and Hope added a cake she'd made. Georgie had brought loads of sandwiches and some samosas she'd got from the supermarket, and Charlotte had brought a couple of posh bottles of cider she'd stolen from her mum's fridge. Nate's contribution was some paper plates and plastic cutlery he'd 'borrowed' from the canteen – and a bottle of champagne he'd hung back to buy from the newsagents when we weren't looking.

'Why not?' JB said. 'I've only got English this afternoon. Bit of booze won't hurt when it comes to getting through *Lear*.'

'I'll drink to that,' Nate said, popping the cork. 'Hope Hunter lets me read Cordelia again.'

Hope flopped onto her side, breaking off a bit of brownie. 'I don't. You were rubbish last time.'

'So you're eighteen, JB,' Charlotte said, stretching out in the sun. 'How's it feel to be a grown-up?'

JB took the bottle Nate was offering him and took a swig. 'If being a grown-up means drinking champagne at twelve thirty on a Tuesday, I'm in.'

We ended up staying there for hours, skipping the afternoon's lessons. It wasn't like me, but then I wasn't exactly feeling like *me* that week at all. And there was something lovely about lying there in the middle of the field, just us, like nothing else existed. Talking about silly stuff, nothingy stuff, watching the thinnest wisps of cloud drift slowly across the sky.

'Ha!' I rolled onto my front and clicked onto an article in the search results I'd just pulled up. 'I knew it. Here we go: "Nutella was invented in Italy during World War Two." I told you it wasn't American!'

'All right, fair,' Nate said. 'You win, Miss Lin.'

'For that piece of useless knowledge, you get the last brownie, Dais,' JB said, leaning over to pass it to me. I reached out to take it, barely noticing my phone vibrating on the blanket beside me.

JB noticed though. I glanced down just in time to see the message he'd already read.

```
Nice tits! Send me a pic? ;)
```

Grant Tyrell from the rugby team.

I flipped the phone over, turned to Charlotte. 'So are you going to message Billy about this party then?'

But when the conversation moved on, I kept catching JB watching me. A thoughtful look on his face. A worried look. I tried to smile at him, tried to keep the conversation moving. It was his birthday, and everything felt better and I wanted it to stay that way.

At about three thirty Nate went into town and came back with more sweets and crisps – we were all sun-lazy by then, full of cake and cheese and not wanting the afternoon to end. Charlotte was on a sugar-high, in the middle of loudly detailing exactly what she liked about Billy Butler, when Nate, laughing, interrupted.

'Jesus, Char, you sound like the female version of Zack.'

'Or Gordon,' JB said, shaking his head.

'Urgh, don't mention that man to me,' Hope said, rolling onto her side and swigging the last dregs in her can. 'I still can't believe the nerve he had turning up the other night.'

My heart turned to ice in my chest even though there wasn't a cloud in the sky.

'Turning up where?' Nate asked, sitting up.

'At Daisy's . . .' Hope trailed off, realising halfway through that I hadn't told any of the others.

'He did *what*?' JB asked, his face turning hard.

I felt all of their eyes on me, a cool breeze lifting the grass around us. 'Oh, it was nothing,' I tried to say. 'I guess he heard about the rumours.'

'He was trying to shut you up,' Hope said quietly.

I was silent then, looking down at the weave of the blanket.

'I can't fucking believe this,' Nate said, but everyone else was quiet too.

'Can we just not talk about it?' I asked. 'We were having such a nice afternoon.'

'But, Daisy –' Georgie started, but JB put a hand on her shoulder and she stopped.

'Dais is right,' he said. 'Let's not let the Conways ruin this. Anyone up for a game of cards?'

THE SUN WAS setting by the time I got home, still warm with sugar and heat. The battery on my phone had finally given up at about 4 p.m. and I felt light, unanchored in some way. I felt like things were OK again.

And then I rounded the corner onto my street, and saw Logan standing outside my front door.

'Hi,' he said, and we both stood and looked at each other.

'Hi.'

'Can I come in?'

The hallway was dark after a day outside and I had to blink to get my eyes to adjust. I turned away from Logan, hanging my jacket on the banister, glad my parents were out for dinner that night. Conscious of being close to him in that small space, of all the times he'd walked through that door and into my arms. I took a step back, trying to push the thoughts away.

'Do you want a drink?'

He gave me a small smile. 'Cup of tea would be good.'

I waited for the kettle to boil while he sat at the kitchen table, looking down at his hands.

'How have you been?' he asked.

'I've been sad,' I said. 'But I'm doing OK. How are you?'

I set his tea down in front of him and then retreated to the other side of the table, not sure how close I should be.

'I need to talk to you about something,' he said. 'I didn't know who else to go to.'

'OK.' My heart beat against my chest like it might burst free.

'It's Hope,' he said. The very last two words I'd expected to emerge.

'Hope?'

'I know you two have got close lately . . .' He reached out to pick up his tea and then changed his mind, wrapping his hands round it instead. 'I guess she's probably told you about Emily.'

I nodded.

'The thing is, I've kept in touch with Ness. It's been eating me up, Daisy. Thinking about how I let Hope down, how I let you down . . . And then there was Emily. I guess it all got muddled up in my head. I wanted to help, *do* something.'

'OK.' My pulse was slowing, the panic fading. 'That doesn't sound so bad.'

For the first time he looked up from the table, his eyes locking on mine. 'Emily's dead, Dais.'

I felt like I'd been punched. 'What? How do you know?'

'Ness called me this morning. She's in bits.'

'But . . . Oh my God. What happened?'

'They're not sure, but they finally found the bloke's car she was seen getting in. It had gone off a cliff. It had sunk, they'd probably never have found them – but some fishing boat went off course during a storm and saw a bit of the bumper floating there.'

'Oh, Logan.' I reached out and took his hand, and he squeezed mine back.

'They reckon the guy was drunk, trying to impress her. Just drove straight off the fucking cliff.'

'That's so awful.'

'I know.' He rubbed a hand over his face. 'I know it's stupid to be upset. I only met the girl once, for fucksake. I just feel so bad for her family, her mates. Like I said, it's kind of got muddled in my head.'

'It's OK to be upset,' I said. 'It's all right to care.'

He sighed, looking up at me again. His hand was still warm in mine. 'Ness asked if she should call Hope, and I said no. I said I'd tell her.'

I nodded. 'I think that was the right thing to say. She's going to be upset too.'

'Now I wish I'd bottled it,' he said. 'I know it really bothered her, what happened. That's why she stopped messaging Ness. I think she thought . . .' He trailed off, eyes on the table again.

'She told me about the night of the booze cruise,' I said. 'She's not mad at you, you know.'

'She should be.'

'Maybe. But she's not.'

He was silent again for a while.

'Are you?'

I thought about it. 'Maybe frustrated. But no. I don't think anyone's as mad with you as you are.'

He let out a soft little laugh. 'Yeah, you're probably right.'

I let go of his hand and picked up my tea, taking a shaky sip. 'I'm glad you're here,' I said.

* * *

We talked for a long time, Logan and I. We talked about little things – about the book I was writing, about the exams he'd decided to retake. And we talked about the more important stuff: about how things had been for me, about how he'd been feeling. About how he was finally talking.

'Steph's on my case,' he told me. 'She checks in like twice a day.'

'That's good,' I said. 'You've got a lovely family, Lo. Let them help you.'

He was quiet then. 'I'm sorry,' he said eventually. 'What happened with Zack . . . I should've been there.'

'You shouldn't have needed to be.'

'Afterwards, I mean. I should've spoken to you. I just . . . I felt like you were better off without me. That sounds so pathetic now.'

'Well, you're here. And I'm here for you, you know.'

It was fully dark outside, the kitchen clock ticking past ten. My parents would be home soon, would be wondering what Logan was doing there. But I didn't care. I still felt warm from the day, from the tea, from having him there and from all of these words spilling out between us.

And then his phone rang.

'Probably Steph,' he said, reaching round the back of the chair to pull it out of his jacket pocket. But when he checked the screen, he was wrong.

'All right, Nate?' he said, answering.

And then he listened, his face changing.

'We'll be right there,' he said.

WE ARRIVED AT the hospital twenty-five minutes later. I almost thought Logan was going to run the whole way there, but we got as far as the main road before finding a taxi to flag down.

Past the sliding doors, the hospital smelled of antiseptic and bleach, something else metallic. A cleaner pulled a mop slowly across the speckled vinyl floor and a little girl sat on her mum's lap, crying.

Logan strode over to the reception desk, me hurrying after him.

'We need to see JB . . . no, sorry, Jonathan Brown,' Logan said, his fingers gripping the edge of the counter.

'Are you family?' the receptionist asked, hands moving quickly over her keyboard.

'We're his friends,' I said. 'Please.'

'Daisy!'

We both turned at the sound of my name. Hope was standing in the mouth of the corridor, still in her outfit from school but with her feet shoved into UGG-style slippers and her hair pulled up in an untidy knot.

'Oh my God.' I ran over to her, skidding on the wet floor, Logan close behind me. 'Is he OK? What the hell happened?'

'He's through here,' Hope said, and I saw how puffy and red her eyes were. 'He's a mess, guys.'

We followed her through a set of double doors and into a ward, hushed voices and bleeping machines, two nurses shushing past in blue scrubs. Hope padded across to a bay, pushing back the curtain, and Logan and I followed her. I felt like I couldn't breathe.

Nate was sitting beside the bed, his hand on the mattress holding JB's.

And JB.

Well, you remember.

One eye swollen shut, a storm of purple clouding the side of his face. Dried blood around his nose and mouth, his jaw jutting at a strange angle.

'Oh, mate,' Logan said, slipping past me and going to the other side of the bed, squeezing JB's other hand. His voice thick as he asked: 'Who did this?'

Hope and I stood at the end of the bed, her arm round me.

And out the story came.

You already know it of course.

HERE'S HOW IT GOES:
He knocks on your door a little after seven. Too many beers, too many circling thoughts, words he's decided he has to let out. He stands on your doorstep and tells you that what you are doing is wrong. That the messages I'm receiving from your friends are wrong. That cutting him out of your life because of his sexuality is wrong.

He says you say nothing.
    He says you seem ashamed.
    But when he's done speaking, he says you ask him to leave.
    'It's your life,' you say. 'But I can't be around it.'
    He's upset, he's drunk. He tells you again that you are wrong. He tells you this loudly.
    Loud enough that your brother and your dad come out to see what's going on.
    They tell him to leave too. They laugh at his tears.
    And you laugh right along with them.

And then, when he's walking home in the growing dark, three sets of footsteps follow him.
    Your brother and his friends.
    Who found they had something to say to him after all.

WHEN JB FINISHED telling his story, Nate stood up, suddenly, like he couldn't bear to have the words near him.

'I'm going round there.'

'Don't,' Logan said, quietly. His hand still held JB's. 'Don't give them the satisfaction, Nate. Let the police handle it instead – it'll hurt them far more.'

Nate snorted but he sat back down. 'I'd like to see Freddie go back to Oxford once he's done for a hate crime.'

I sank down onto the end of the bed, resting a hand on JB's foot. 'What do you need, babe?'

He smiled at me, wincing with the effort. 'We can't get hold of Georgie. Can you try her again? Mum and David are still on their flight.'

'Yeah, sure –' I found my phone in my bag, turned to leave. But the curtain was already being pulled back, someone else stepping in.

And, of course, it was you.

It was Hope who moved first, her eyes flashing angrily. 'Get out,' she said, blocking your way, her voice trembling. 'Get out of here right now, Zack.'

'Fuck,' you said, your eyes on JB. 'Mate, I –'

'He is not your mate,' Nate growled. 'Hope's right. You need to leave.'

286

'I didn't know . . .' You were stammering, your face pale. I'd never seen you so lost, so uncertain.

I almost felt sorry for you.

Almost.

And then your eyes locked on me. 'Daisy, I –'

'You should leave,' I told you, and my hands were shaking.

Logan got up from his place beside the bed. 'You heard them, Zack,' he said, walking round towards you. 'It's time to go.'

'Lo . . . JB . . . I swear I didn't know they were gonna –'

'That's not the point, Zack,' Logan said. 'You started this. And you can't fix it.'

'Lo, please.' Your voice cracked, and we all held our breath. Everything was cracking. 'It's my dad,' you said. 'He puts pressure on me. He expects me to be a certain way, you know. It's always been like that, since we were kids. He's always telling me I've got to be a man, can't let the side down.'

'Don't do that.' The words left my mouth before I realised I'd thought them. 'Don't blame other people.'

'Please, Zack.' JB's voice was muffled through the swelling, through the gauze they'd pushed into his cheek to stop the bleeding from a tooth your brother's friend cracked with a fist. 'Just go.'

And you looked at him, at each of us.

Then you turned and you left.

But not before I saw the first tear fall.

AND HERE WE are, Zack. One year on. Another plane, another blue sky.

And everything has changed.

We've had an early start, and Hope leans her head against my shoulder, sleepily flicking through a magazine she bought at the gate.

'You guys hungry?' JB, on the end, offering out the Haribo he picked up there too.

His face looks better, finally. There's still a small scar near his jaw, left by a fragment of stone as someone stamped his head into the ground. His nose is ever so slightly crooked, though only he can tell, can point out where the break happened.

But he's good. We haven't even taken off yet, and already he's got his phone out, sending a message to Paul, the boy from Southfield he met at an end-of-sixth-form party we went to a couple of weeks ago. Somehow I think we'll be seeing more of him this summer.

'I'll have some,' Nate says, pushing his head between Hope and JB's seats. He's ended up next to Charlotte and Georgie, who are already planning where they want to go tonight, poring over Georgie's guidebook and poking each other in excitement.

Nate's playing along for now, but I've got a feeling he's hungover from last night and would rather put in his earphones and get some sleep.

He's been brilliant, you know. To all of us. It was him who suggested this holiday, who did all the research and collected deposits. It's him who's kept on at Logan to talk to him, to go on jogs round the park or – this will surprise you – to play a round of golf on a Saturday morning. Logan says somehow it's easier to talk that way, in the quiet of the course, both of them walking or taking their shot, eyes on the horizon. So they're talking, they're golfing, and Nate is there for whatever Logan needs him to be there for. For whatever JB needs him to be there for. And for me too.

He even tried to be there for you, didn't he? Him and Logan both, despite everything. After the police had visited, after Freddie and his friends were arrested, after you were questioned, after all of it. They reached out to you. They gave you a chance, remembering, maybe, those tears you shed as you left the hospital.

You didn't return their calls.

You sent a text to Nate: *We're done*. At school you avoided them, all of us. Hung out with your rugby friends, with Emma, your new girlfriend in the year below. You went to Freddie's trial and you watched as your dad's fancy lawyer got him off, as his best friend got sentenced to three years in jail. You got out of your dad's big shiny car every morning until the day you passed your driving test, and then you swung the big shiny car he bought you into a space in the student car park every morning instead.

You chose. I guess we all had to.

'Hey, Dais!' Dev's face appears through the seats to my left, his eyes sliding right to see me. 'You bring the thing?'

'Shh!' I nod. It's Hope's birthday tomorrow; we're planning a surprise birthday party on the beach. Ibiza for your eighteenth – pretty cool, huh? I have a card in my suitcase, pages and pages of messages from all of us, from people at school, photos printed out and glued all over. She's going to love it, and also hate the fact we've made so much effort just for her. I can't wait.

I'm proud of Dev, even though it took me a while to forgive him. He's the most dedicated of us, now he's decided what it is he wants to do. It's weird, isn't it – it seems so obvious now that he'd be a brilliant primary-school teacher. I guess I didn't realise how much he loved his cousins' kids, how he babysat them a lot of the time. Maybe he didn't realise that was a path for him, but now he does, he's taking it seriously. He was the first to get his UCAS application in, and he's the only one who has plans after we get back next week – he's off to Spain, his TEFL course finished months ago.

'You guys want Pringles?' he asks now, removing his face from the gap to stick the tube through, his head appearing above the seat. 'They're smoky bacon, so basically breakfast-flavoured.'

'Yeah, all right.' Hope leans forward to take a stack, but I'm too excited and nervous to eat. Lame as it might sound, this is my first real holiday – in my head at least. My parents took me to visit my dad's family in Singapore when I was a kid but I barely remember it, and since then it's always been a long weekend in Devon or a trip up to Scotland to visit Grandma. I love all of that, but this feels different. This feels grown-up and real, and I'm so happy that I'm here with all of these people that I love.

'You guys are gross.' And there's Logan, in the aisle seat next to Dev. Slightly queasy-looking like he always is first thing in the morning – remember? Grumpy because he fell asleep at the gate and had to be woken up by JB when boarding was called. But he's smiling. He's doing well. We're all getting there.

'Daisy, promise me I won't have to sleep near any breakfast-crisp-eaters,' Logan says now, looking towards me, and I laugh.

'Says the man who ate a Mars Bar in the car on the way here.'

'Two,' Hope corrects me, pulling the duty-free catalogue out of the seat pocket in front of her.

The plane judders backwards and starts to turn away from the terminal, the runway unspooling in front of us. 'And we're off!' JB says, claiming a handful of Pringles for himself. 'Ibiza, here we come!'

Logan grins at me, and I smile back.

We're all getting there.

Acknowledgements

Firstly, a huge thank you to Cathryn Summerhayes, who has worked with me on five books now and who has been a complete rockstar every step of the way. Thank you for your endless support and enthusiasm, for championing me, being on my side and making me laugh – truly, I owe you many drinks and all of the cake.

Thank you too to Siobhan O'Neill, who has also been so supportive throughout the writing and publication of this novel.

And to Emma Matthewson, Jane Harris, Tina Mories and Talya Baker at Bonnier – it's been wonderful to see your enthusiasm for each cast of characters I've put in front of you and I'm really happy Hope, Logan and Daisy found a home with you too.

Hayley Richardson: you're still the alpha beta, and I'll never be able to cook you enough fancy dinners to say thanks for that.

And, as always, I've saved the two most important thank yous until last. To Margaret and Richard Cloke, for always being there, for always being incredible, for always reading my manuscripts when they could be enjoying the newest Robert Galbraith or Lee Child instead. You are amazing and I am so lucky to have you. And to Dan Cloke: top brother, fantastic flatmate, excellent friend and seemingly the owner of a well of limitless patience for my ridiculous plot-based questions (which have, over the last few years, covered UK gun law, police ranks, drinking games and football training grounds). He never just tells me to go away and google it (apart from that one time) and he quite rightly complained that he never gets an acknowledgement to himself. Well, here it is, pal. Thanks for being great.

Nicci Cloke

Nicci Cloke is a full-time writer, part-time doer of random jobs. These jobs have included Christmas Elf, cocktail waitress, and childminder. She is also the organiser and host of Speakeasy, the only London literary salon to host regular YA events. Her first YA novel, FOLLOW ME BACK, was published in 2016 and was nominated for the 2017 CILIP Carnegie Medal, longlisted for the Branford Boase Award 2017 and shortlisted for the Lancashire Book of the Year Award 2017. Her next YA novel is CLOSE YOUR EYES, published in 2017. TOXIC is her third novel for young adults. Her first adult novel SOMEDAY FIND ME was published by Fourth Estate in 2012 and her second LAY ME DOWN was published by Cape in 2014. Her most recent adult novel is THE TALL MAN. Follow Nicci on Twitter: @niccicloke.

Have you read Nicci Cloke's first book?

Nominated for the
CILIP Carnegie Medal 2017

Out now in paperback and ebook.

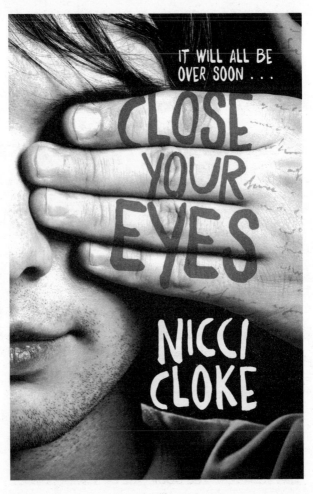

HOT KEY BOOKS

Thank you for choosing a Hot Key book.

If you want to know more about our authors and what we publish, you can find us online.

You can start at our website

www.hotkeybooks.com

And you can also find us on:

We hope to see you soon!